DEATH SENTENCE

"You *don't* know who Clint Adams is?" Lisa said. "The Gunsmith, Nancy," Lisa said, "the damned *Gun*smith, that's what *I'm* referring to."

Nancy stopped short and stared at Lisa. "The Gunsmith?"

"*Now* you know who he is?"

"Are you sure?" Nancy asked.

"Of course I'm sure," Lisa said. "He's the man who's gonna destroy Freedom for us, that's who he is."

Nancy shook her head and said, "I don't see it, Lisa. Why should he?"

"Look," Lisa said, "years ago, before he became who he is now, he was a lawman—and once a lawman, always a lawman, I say. Nancy, we built this up, you and I, and he's gonna bring us down."

"What did we build that's so great, Lisa?" Nancy asked. "What?"

"A world without men, that's what."

"What do you propose we do, then, Lisa?"

"What else?" Lisa said. "Kill him."

*   *   *

SPECIAL PREVIEW!
Turn to the back of this book for a special excerpt from the next exciting western by Giles Tippette . . .

Dead Man's Poker

. . .The riveting story of a former outlaw's biggest gamble, by America's new star of the classic western.
Available now from Jove Books!

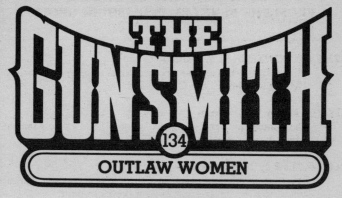

THE GUNSMITH

134

OUTLAW WOMEN

J. R. ROBERTS

JOVE BOOKS, NEW YORK

OUTLAW WOMEN

A Jove Book / published by arrangement with
the author

PRINTING HISTORY
Jove edition / February 1993

All rights reserved.
Copyright © 1993 by Jove Publications, Inc.
Excerpt from *Dead Man's Poker* copyright © 1993 by Giles Tippette.
This book may not be reproduced in whole
or in part, by mimeograph or any other means,
without permission. For information address:
The Berkley Publishing Group, 200 Madison Avenue,
New York, New York 10016.

ISBN: 0-515-11045-0

Jove Books are published by The Berkley Publishing Group,
200 Madison Avenue, New York, New York 10016.
The name "JOVE" and the "J" logo
are trademarks belonging to Jove Publications, Inc.

PRINTED IN THE UNITED STATES OF AMERICA

10 9 8 7 6 5 4 3 2 1

ONE

Benbow, Kansas, was a quiet town—at least, it had been up until that morning.

Clint Adams had ridden into Benbow with his rig, looking forward to some nice quiet hours repairing guns, playing poker, and perhaps dallying with a lady. Many a time in the past those had been Clint's intentions, but things hadn't turned out that way. However, for two weeks now in Benbow, things had turned out *exactly* that way.

Clint woke that morning with a pleasant weight on his left arm. He turned his head and looked at the sleeping face of Brenda Carlson. Brenda was blond and slender. Hell, she was skinny, skinnier than Clint usually liked his women, but there was something else about Brenda that attracted him to her. She had been working the saloon with three other girls that first night, and truth be told, the other three girls were all prettier, in one way or another. So it wasn't Brenda's appearance that had attracted him. It was something in the way she carried herself, something in the way she cocked her head when she asked if she could get him anything. There was *something* just downright

1

straightforward about her. There was no false coquet-
tishness, like there was with the other girls, no games,
no flirtatious looks. When you looked at Brenda, and
spoke to her, you got what you saw and heard. She was
honest.

He examined her profile now. Her nose was kind of
sharp, and her jaw angular. When you looked at her
head-on you saw wide, clear blue eyes, a slender nose,
and a wide, slim-lipped mouth. She didn't have the
kind of face that had men thinking about biting her
mouth right away, but when she smiled her face was
transformed. Her smile was incredibly wide and *white*,
and when she laughed it came from deep down inside.
He was looking forward to her waking up, because
when those eyes opened and her mouth smiled, for
him it was like looking at a spring day.

He eased his arm out from beneath her without waking her, and gently turned the sheet down from her
neck to her waist. Now he could see her breasts. They
were small, and when she was lying on her back like
that they were almost *gone.* Her nipples, though—
well, she had the biggest, widest nipples he had ever
seen, and they were *sensitive.* He leaned over now and
touched one nipple with the tip of his tongue, and she
reacted immediately. She moaned and stretched her
body taut, her arms going up over her head. He drew
the nipple into his mouth then, and started to suckle
it. She moaned again, but this time she was awake,
and her hands came down to cup his head and caress
the back of his neck while he sucked first one nipple
and then the other.

"You're gettin' me all worked up," she said, her tone
like a warning. "You do that and you ain't gonna be
gettin' out of this bed for a while."

He looked up at her, smiled, and said, "I've got no place to go in a hurry."

He straddled her then and lowered his mouth to her belly, laving her navel with his tongue, leaving a wet path behind him as he worked his way down between her legs. She spread her slender thighs wide and stretched again, and when he poked his tongue into her it was as if lightning had come down from the sky and struck her.

"Ooh!" she said, her buttocks jumping up off the bed.

He slid his hands beneath her to cup her thin buttocks, and began moving his tongue over her in long, slow strokes.

"Oh, God," she groaned, "Jesus in Heaven . . . you've got a magic tongue . . ."

He closed his mouth on her and sucked, and suddenly she was bucking beneath him, her slim body wracked by waves of pleasure that were almost unbearable. She started to beat her fists on his back, but they had been through this before and he knew she wasn't trying to beat him *away* from her, or get him off her. She simply *had* to pound on something . . .

After she had settled down he slid up onto her, just poking at her moist portal with the spongy head of his penis.

"Jesus," she said, "that *almost* feels too good. I mean, can someone *die* from feeling too good?"

"I don't think so," he said.

"Good," she said, putting her arms around him and lifting and spreading her knees. "Then make me feel good some more."

He drove into her then and she gasped, tightened her knees on him, and caught her bottom lip between her teeth. Of course, he thought, if she happened to bite her lip off she *could* bleed to death, but he was too busy at that moment to mention it to her . . .

She watched him while he dressed, and asked, "When are you leaving?"

She had asked him that question the past three mornings in a row, as if she could sense that the time when he would leave was drawing nearer and nearer. In truth, if it were not for Brenda, he might have left Benbow days ago.

"Maybe a few days," he said.

"You say that every day."

"Then stop asking every day," he said, kissing the tip of her nose.

"I can't help it," she said, lying back on the bed. She put her hands over her head and stared at the ceiling. "I know the day is coming, and there's nothing I can do about it."

"Then don't worry about it either, Brenda," he said. "When it comes, it comes."

"I know, I know," she said. "It's just that . . . I'd like to know when our last night together is so I can make sure we both enjoy it as much as we possibly can."

He smiled at her, leaned over, and kissed both of her breasts, lingering long enough that she closed her eyes and sighed.

"We enjoy *every* night that way," he whispered to her breasts, nuzzling them with his nose.

She smiled, stretched still again, and said dreamily, "Yeah, we do, don't we?"

"Get some more rest," he said, standing up straight. "We were up late last night, and woke up early this morning."

"*You* kept me up late, and *you* woke me up early," she reminded him.

"I know," he said, heading for the door, "and I feel terribly guilty about it."

While he was going out the door he heard her say behind him, "Like hell you do."

She was right.

TWO

Although they had spent most of his nights in Benbow together, Clint and Brenda had taken very few meals with each other—and they had *never* had breakfast together. Brenda was used to sleeping past noon, because she always worked right up until closing time at the saloon.

Clint had taken to having breakfast at a nearby small cafe, rather than in the hotel dining room. With all the traveling he had done and all the towns he had been in, it was his experience that the smaller the place, the more attention they gave to the food, and to each customer. This particular cafe boasted only six tables, and the service *and* food were equally good. If he had any complaint, it would have been that the coffee could have been a *little* stronger. Still, that was a minor quibble when the food was so good.

"Morning, Mr. Adams," Mrs. Quinn said in greeting as he walked in. Hattie Quinn did all the serving and her husband, Harold, did all the cooking. It was an arrangement that they *and* their customers agreed worked to perfection.

"Good morning, Mrs. Quinn."

"The usual today?" she asked.

"Yes, please."

The "usual" was four scrambled eggs, a side of bacon, a mound of potatoes, biscuits, and coffee. Clint knew he was getting too old to eat that way every day, but his *appetite* was the same as it had been twenty years ago. Ah, well, maybe he'd cut back to three eggs . . .

Down the street Walter Miller, the manager of the Benbow Bank, was just unlocking the front door from inside when it was suddenly pushed open. It struck him in the center of the forehead, and he staggered backward a few steps, seeing stars for a moment. When his vision cleared he found himself looking at three masked figures. One was tall and slender, and the other two were short. He squinted, wondering if he was seeing correctly. They all seemed to have hats on that were too big for them. In fact, the hats were pulled down almost over their ears, and their faces were masked with kerchiefs.

"What is the meaning of this?" he demanded.

"Shut up," the tall one said. His voice was muffled by the mask, but it sounded more like the voice of a young boy rather than that of an older man.

Behind Mr. Miller the two tellers were looking on wide-eyed. One was a man in his twenties who wore very thick eyeglasses, and the other a woman in her fifties who was barely five feet tall. The man adjusted his eyeglasses and peered myopically at what was transpiring. The woman was trying to sink down behind her teller's cage, which was not hard for someone of her height.

One of the other robbers turned, locked the door, and pulled the shade down.

"Move," the taller one said to Miller.

"Is this a holdup?" he demanded, his voice going so high it almost squeaked.

"That's right."

"Oh, dear."

The taller of the three robbers pushed him and said, "Get behind the cages with the others."

All three robbers were holding guns. One of them stayed by the front door, peering out from behind the shade, while the other two moved to the cages with Miller. Miller found their clothes as strange as their hats. They seemed to be wearing clothing that was also too big for them. One of them had a piece of rope around his waist, cinched very tight around an almost impossibly small waist for a man. Again, Miller was struck at how they resembled boys more than men. Could it be that the bank was being held up by boys in their teens?

"Put the money in a sack," the taller one said. "Hurry!"

"Do as he says," Miller said to the two tellers.

"Mr. Miller," the myopic man said, "we should call the sheriff."

"Very good, Leon," Miller said. "Why don't you go and do that?"

Leon looked at the two robbers with the guns, then back at his boss.

"Me? B-b-but they'll shoot me."

"Then shut up and fill the sack!"

Miller looked at the taller of the robbers and shook his head. The robber simply shrugged, as if sympathizing with him.

"Here," the female teller said, holding the sack out to Miller.

Miller took it, turned to the robbers, and said, "Here."

The second robber took it.

"Now the safe," the taller one said.

"Oh, no," Miller said, but he turned to the safe and started to open it with no further prompting.

"Fill another sack," the tall robber said.

"Leon, help me," Miller said.

"S-sir?"

"Help me!"

"I'll help," the woman said.

"Thank you, Rose."

The woman—whose name was Rose Tyler—helped Miller fill the second sack, which he then handed to the second robber. The second robber had tossed the first sack to the third robber, who was still watching the door.

The taller robber cocked the hammer on his gun, and the three bank people all jumped at the sound.

"Nobody steps outside for ten minutes. Understand?"

"We understand," Miller assured the robber.

The first two robbers backed up until they were standing with the third robber. That one unlocked the door and all three went outside.

Across the street from the bank Sheriff Sam Cornell thought it odd that the shade on the bank was drawn when the bank should have been opened ten minutes ago. Cornell, a man in his fifties who had intentions of retiring soon, decided to cross over and see what was happening. It was at that point the three robbers came out of the bank, almost face-to-face with the lawman.

"Jesus," Cornell said, and pulled his gun.

THREE

Clint was pouring what was to be his last cup of coffee—at breakfast, that is—when he heard the shots from down the street.

"Damn," he said softly. He knew the peace and quiet had been too good to be true. If he had left a few days ago . . .

Well, there was no point in thinking like that.

He stood up and ran to the door. The shots were still being fired, so he ran outside, located them, and ran in that direction. Sure, he could have stayed where he was and finished his coffee—but that would have made him a completely different man.

As he was running it became obvious that the shots were coming from the bank. As he reached the area he saw three riders fleeing up the street. There was a man in the street, down on one knee, firing after them. By the time he reached the man it was too late for Clint to do anything but help him up.

"Damn it," the man said, shaking off Clint's hand.

"Easy," Clint said.

"They just robbed the bank, damn it!" the man said. "I've got to go after them."

The man turned towards Clint, and he had just enough time to see the badge on the man's chest before the lawman starting falling towards him. Clint caught him, and felt the man's sticky blood on his hands.

"Sheriff!" a man shouted, coming out of the bank. "Get after them!"

"I'm afraid he can't do that," Clint said, looking over his shoulder. "Would you mind getting a doctor, please?"

"B-but they're getting away," the man said.

"Get a doctor . . . now!" Clint shouted.

Clint waited in the street outside the doctor's office with a deputy who had introduced himself as Hal Clemens. He was a young man, in his early or mid-twenties, and he was obviously extremely concerned about the sheriff's condition.

The wound had been in the torso, as far as Clint could see. He had not had time to determine how serious it might be. They were now waiting to hear about it from the doctor.

"Deputy," Miller, the bank manager, said. "Those robbers are getting away."

"Mr. Miller," Clemens said, facing the manager. "As soon as I know about the sheriff's condition I'll get out after them with a posse."

"B-but they're getting further and further away," Miller complained.

"There'll still be a trail to follow, Mr. Miller," Clemens said. "I suggest you get back to the bank and figure out how much they got away with. I'll be along shortly to ask you and your employees some questions."

"Deputy—"

"That's all, Mr. Miller."

Miller stared at the deputy for a long moment, but the deputy refused to avert his eyes, and eventually Miller backed off and started for the bank.

Deputy Hal Clemens heaved a sigh of relief at the bank manager's retreating back.

"You did all right," Clint said.

"Thanks," Clemens said, but before he could say anything else the doctor stepped out of his office. He was a tall, gangly-looking man, gray-haired, in his sixties. He had the complexion of a heavy drinker. Clint wondered *how* heavy.

"How is he, Doc?" Clemens asked.

"He took a bullet in the left side," the doctor said. "It might have nicked a rib. He's in pain, but he'll be all right. He, uh, won't be leading any posses for a while, though."

"No," Deputy Clemens said, "I guess that's gonna be *my* job."

"Then I suggest you get to it," the doctor said, and went back into his office. "I'm gonna get back to mine, and then go get me a drink. Stitchin' people up is thirsty work."

As the doctor went back inside the deputy turned to Clint. They had made their introductions while waiting outside the doctor's office, so the deputy knew who Clint Adams was.

"Mr. Adams," Clemens said. "Will you ride with the posse?"

Clint had been afraid of that, and he was ready with his answer. He had already decided that he would not be pulled into the troubles of Benbow, Kansas.

"I'm afraid I can't, Deputy," Clint said. "I'll be leaving town tomorrow."

"Tomorrow?"

"That's right," Clint said, and added to himself, "Before anything *else* can happen."

"Well, I can't say as I blame you," Clemens said, rubbing his jaw. "This ain't your home. But can I ask you a favor?"

"Sure," Clint said, "go ahead and ask."

"Will you come over to the bank with me? There might be some questions I'll forget to ask that a man of your experience might remember."

"Sure," Clint said again, "I can do that."

"Thanks," the deputy said. "Let's go."

FOUR

"So none of you saw their faces?" Deputy Hal Clemens said.

"I already told you that, Deputy," Miller said. "You should be out there looking for those bank robbers."

"I'm gonna do that, Mr. Miller," Clemens said patiently, "but when I catch them I'd like to be able to recognize them."

"Well, I told you they wore masks," Miller said, "but I know one thing."

"Oh? And what's that?"

"They weren't men."

"They weren't?"

"No," Miller said haughtily, "that much was obvious to a man as observant as I am."

"I see," Clemens said, exchanging glances with Clint. "Well, if they weren't men—"

"They were boys," Miller said, "mere boys dressed up as men."

"And what makes you say that, sir?" Clemens asked.

"Well, the way they were dressed, of course," Miller said. "Their clothing was too big, as were their hats—and the one who spoke? He did not have a deep

14

voice. It was the voice of a boy in his teens. Yes, sir, Deputy, you are looking for boys in their teens if you ask me."

"I see," Clemens said. He looked at Clint again, but Clint wasn't looking at either him or Miller. He was looking at Rose Tyler, who seemed to have something to say, but was afraid to say it.

"What about you, ma'am?" Clint asked.

"What?" she said.

"What did you see?"

"What do you mean, what did she see?" Miller asked. "She saw the same thing I saw, of course."

"Is that right, ma'am?" Clint asked.

"Who is he?" Miller asked Clemens, but the deputy ignored him.

"Do you have something to tell us, Rose?" Clemens asked the woman.

"Well . . . yes, I do," she said. Now that she had been asked she seemed emboldened. "It was very clear to me that those robbers were not men—"

"See?" Miller said.

"—or boys," she went on undaunted.

"Then what were they, Rose?" Clemens asked.

"Well, they were women of course," she said.

"What?" Clemens said.

"Women?" Clint said.

"Impossible!" Miller said.

"I could tell by the way they moved," Rose Tyler said. "Just as Mr. Miller said, they were wearing clothes too big for them, but they were women, all right."

"What makes you so sure, Rose?" Clemens asked. "Could you tell some other way than just by the way they moved?"

"This is preposterous!" Miller said, but no one was paying any attention to him.

"The skin," Rose Tyler said. "I could see their skin, from their noses to the brims of their hats. And also their hands. Only a woman has skin like that. And then there was the smell."

"What about it?"

"They *smelled* like women," she said.

Suddenly, Miller felt very uncomfortable. There *had* been something about the way they smelled, now that Rose Tyler mentioned it.

"All right," Clemens said. "Thanks, everyone. I'll be goin' out with a posse to find them." He and Clint turned to leave, and then Clemens turned back and asked, "You wouldn't want to come out with the posse, would you, Mr. Miller?"

"What? Me?" Miller squeaked.

"I didn't think so," the deputy said, and followed Clint out.

"What did you think?" Clemens asked Clint outside.

"I'd put more faith in what the lady said than in what the bank manager said," Clint replied. "Or am I reading the man wrong?"

"You're reading him right," Clemens said. "So I'm looking for three lady bank robbers?"

"Looks that way."

"I never heard of such a thing."

Clint almost said he hadn't either, but then again he knew three lady bounty hunters, so why not lady bank robbers?

"You learn something new every day," he said instead.

"Ain't that true," Clemens said. "Well, I got to get that posse put together."

"You might want to talk to the sheriff before you do that," Clint said. "He might remember something helpful."

"I'll do that," Clemens said. "Thanks for your help, Mr. Adams."

"Glad to do what I can, Deputy."

"Uh, sure you wouldn't want to ride along?" Clemens asked.

"I'm afraid not, Deputy," Clint said.

"Just thought I'd ask one more time," Clemens said.

"If I don't see you before I leave," Clint said, "good luck."

"Thanks," Clemens said. "I'll need it. This'll be the first posse I lead."

"There's always a first one, Deputy."

Clint watched the young man walk away and—just for a moment—almost called out to him, but refrained from doing so. For once—just for *once*—he was going to mind his own business.

FIVE

That afternoon Clint went to the livery stable and checked over his team, his rig, and his big black gelding, Duke, to make sure they were in condition to travel. The liveryman offered to do it for him, but Clint insisted on examining his stock himself.

When he finished with that he went to the general store to stock up on supplies. While he was there he heard the store clerk—who was also probably the owner of the store—talking with another man.

"You goin' out on that posse?" the other man asked.

"I got to," the clerk said. "My money was in that bank."

"My money's under my mattress," the other man said. "Glad I don't have to ride with that deputy in charge. You know what he's been sayin'?"

"You mean about the bank robbers bein' women?" the storekeeper asked.

"Ain't that the silliest thing you ever heard?" the man asked. He shook his head and said, "Glad I ain't followin' him after three bank robbers, I tell you that right now."

"Why don't you give the man a chance?" Clint said

before he had a chance to stop himself.

Both men looked at him and said, "What's it to you, stranger?"

This time Clint was able to gain control of himself before he got into an argument.

"Nothing," he said, shaking his head, "nothing at all. Can I get some supplies?"

The other man left, and the storekeeper took Clint's list and filled it, all the time giving him funny looks.

"When's the posse going out?" Clint asked.

"Tomorrow morning," the man said. "Why?"

"Just curious," Clint said. He paid the man, took his supplies, and left.

He went back to the livery and stowed his supplies on his rig, then left the livery and walked over to the saloon. It was late afternoon and the girls were already working. Brenda saw him as soon as he entered and gave him a smile.

He went to the bar and ordered a beer, then drank it while he listened to a conversation between the bartender and two other men. It seemed they also thought the deputy was crazy, but the two of them still felt compelled to ride with the posse.

"Me," one of them said, "I don't care if we're hunting men, boys, or women. They got my money, and I'm gonna get them."

"String 'em up as soon as we catch 'em," the other man said.

"I'd go if I could," the bartender said, "but I gotta work."

"Sure, Dave, sure," the other man said, and they both left laughing.

"Did you hear that?" Dave the bartender said to Clint.

"What?"

"Posse's goin' out after some women, they say. *Women* holdin' up a bank."

"Why not?"

"Huh?"

"Why couldn't it happen?" Clint asked the man.

The bartender gave him a look like he was crazy and said, "You want another beer?"

"Not yet."

Dave moved down to the other end of the bar and started talking to somebody else about female bank robbers. It was good for a laugh.

Brenda came over to Clint and said, "I heard what happened."

"So did I."

"Did you hear what they're sayin'?" she asked. "The deputy thinks the bank was held up by three women."

"I heard."

"You believe that?"

"Sure," he said. "Don't you think three women would be smart enough and brave enough to rob a bank?"

"Well . . ." she said, and then with a shrug said, "Sure, why not?"

"Right," he said, "why not?"

"You're not ridin' with the posse, are you?" she asked.

"No," he said. "I was asked, but no . . . I am leaving, though."

"Leavin' town?"

"Yes."

"When?"

"In the morning."

"Damn," she swore, then shrugged and said, "Oh, well, we still got one night ahead of us, right?"

"That's right."

She stroked his jawline and said, "And it's gonna be a night to remember, I promise."

He watched her walk away, thinking how most of the nights they had spent together had been nights to remember. He was jarred from his reverie by another burst of laughter from the other end of the bar. The bartender was getting a lot of mileage out of the lady-bank-robber story.

"Shit," Clint said, putting his empty mug down on the bar. He *still* wasn't going to ride with the posse, but that didn't mean he couldn't go and talk to the sheriff.

SIX

Clint walked over to the doctor's office and knocked on the door.

"Come on in."

He entered and found himself in a single cluttered room. Against one wall was an examination table. At the moment the doctor was lying on his back on it, balancing a whiskey bottle on his chest—or trying to. It kept falling off, and he kept catching it before it could hit the floor. Clint wondered how long it would be before it *did* hit the floor—or maybe that was the game.

"Doctor?"

"That's who I am," the man on the table said. "The doctor."

Clint searched through his brain for the man's name and came up with it.

"Doctor Russell?"

The doctor turned his head and looked at Clint. At that moment the bottle slid from his chest and headed for the floor. The doctor realized it too late. He reached for it but missed. Clint took two quick steps and caught the bottle one-handed before it hit the floor.

The doctor stared at him and said, "You're fast."

"I'm just not drunk," Clint said, setting the bottle on a nearby flat surface.

"And you think I am?" the doctor asked.

"Aren't you?"

"Sir," the doctor said, "you have obviously never seen me drunk."

The man sat up, swung his legs around to the floor, and stood up. Clint couldn't understand it, but suddenly the man looked completely sober.

"What can I do for you?" Dr. Russell asked him.

"I was looking for the sheriff."

"The sheriff has a small house at the south end of town," the doctor said. "He was carried over there earlier today. That is where he is resting."

"Thanks, Doc."

"You're quite welcome."

Clint stared at the man for a moment, but then decided to leave. The doctor's story would obviously be a long and drawn-out one, and he didn't want to get involved. As he was leaving, though, he saw the man reaching for the bottle.

Clint walked to the south end of town, where a small wood-frame house sat all by itself. He walked to the front door and knocked.

"Come in, damn it!" a voice called.

He entered. The house was apparently only one room, but it was a hell of a lot neater than the doctor's one-room office had been. There was a wooden table with a clean top, and off to the left a small pallet, on which the sheriff was lying on his back.

The man scowled at Clint and asked, "Who are you?"

"My name's Clint Adams," Clint said. "I, uh, was in the street with you today."

"Not soon enough," the man said, and then waved a hand and said, "Forget I said that. I'm just in a bad mood."

"That's understandable."

"I've got three bank robbers on the loose, and one inexperienced deputy to chase them down."

"He's got himself a posse, I hear."

"And how long he'll be able to hold them together is anyone's guess," the sheriff said. "I guess we never got introduced. My name's Sam Cornell. I already know your name. You, uh, didn't come here to say you changed your mind about riding with the posse, did you?"

"No," Clint said firmly, "I didn't."

"Too bad," Cornell said. "The lad could use you."

"He'll do all right," Clint said. "All you've got to do is back him."

"From here?"

"He's apparently told everyone that the bank robbers are three women."

"What?" Cornell said. "What the hell is he telling them that for?"

"Well," Clint said, "for one thing, it's what he and I believe."

Cornell opened his mouth to say something, then shut it and thought a minute.

"You know," he finally said, "I thought there was somethin' funny about those three. That *could* be it, couldn't it?"

"I assume you've put together some posses in the past," Clint said.

"Sure I have."

"So some of the men who'll be riding with Clemens have ridden with you?"

"I'm sure of it," Cornell said. "I usually get the same volunteers."

"Then I have a suggestion for you."

"I'm listening."

"Talk to some of them," Clint said. "Have them back the deputy all the way, and maybe the others will fall into place. The last thing he needs while leading his first posse is a lack of respect."

"That's a good point, Adams," Sheriff Cornell said. "I'll take care of it. Thanks for the suggestion."

"Just looking to help."

"If you're really lookin' to help . . . "

"Don't say it," Clint said. "I'll be leaving in the morning, just like I planned."

"All right," Cornell said. "Thanks anyway for comin' over."

SEVEN

Clint played poker in the saloon until Brenda was ready to leave. She had apparently gotten permission to quit early that night, and when they left the saloon it was still open for business. It was about one in the morning.

They went to Clint's hotel, where they feverishly stripped off their clothes and made love.

"Next time," she said, lying next to him and panting, "we'll go slower."

"Right," he said, also out of breath, "in a little while."

"Well," she said, snaking her hand down over his belly, "*not* such a little while."

"Brenda," he warned her, "I'm an old man."

As his penis stirred beneath her hand she said, "*Not* so old . . ."

He rose with first light the next morning, and Brenda stirred long enough to give him a long, lingering good-bye kiss.

"Remember me," she said sleepily.

"I will," he said, "I promise."

He picked up his rifle and saddlebags and left the room. Downstairs he paid his bill, and then went outside. He started for the livery, but some commotion down the street attracted his attention. He looked that way and saw about a dozen men and horses milling about. Some of the men were mounted, some were not. He decided to take a walk and have a look. He left his saddlebags on a chair in front of the hotel, but carried his rifle.

The men were waiting in front of the sheriff's office, and as Clint reached them the door opened and Deputy Clemens stepped out.

"Is everybody here?" the deputy called out.

"Everybody but Larry Names," someone shouted.

"Should we wait?" Clemens asked.

"Nah," the same voice said, "Names always volunteers, but never gets up early enough to follow through."

"All right then," Clemens said, "let's get moving."

As Clemens stepped down off the boardwalk into the street he saw Clint, and changed direction to meet up with him.

"Morning," the deputy said.

"Good morning, Deputy."

"Gettin' an early start, are you?" Clemens asked.

"Same as you," Clint said, nodding.

"Different direction, though," Clemens said.

That was true. The posse would be heading north, which was the direction the robbers were going when they left town. Clint was going to be heading south.

Clemens lingered a moment, and Clint knew the man was debating whether or not to ask again if he would accompany the posse.

"Well," Clint said, breaking the silence, "good

luck." He stuck his hand out and the deputy shook it firmly.

"Thanks."

Clint watched as the deputy mounted up and led the posse north, out of town.

Clint turned, went back to the hotel, retrieved his saddlebags, and headed for the livery.

He was two days out of Benbow and looking for a place to stop for the night when he saw the fire. Someone was *already* camped and having dinner. Normally, he steered clear of other camps. The years had taught him to be cynical, and he never invaded a stranger's camp. Too many times that had caused him trouble. However, he would have had to deliberately change direction to avoid this camp, and he saw no good reason to do that.

He continued riding, and eventually the camp came into sight. It wasn't much of a camp actually. The fire was close to going out. There was a single figure lying beneath a tree, unmoving. Clint sat his horse a few minutes, watching the camp, and still the figure didn't move. He was either sleeping—or dead.

Slowly, Clint approached the camp, keeping a wary eye out. It could also have been a trap set for unsuspecting and *curious* travelers.

Long before he reached the camp his approach should have been detected. After all, his rig made a lot of noise. Still, the figure in the camp did not stir.

When he reached the camp he dropped down from his rig and looked around. There were some tracks on the ground indicating that once there had been more people there. But right now there was just the one figure—and, he noticed, no horse.

Convinced that he was alone with the figure, he approached it. The figure was lying on the ground, hat over its face, for all intents and purposes dozing—but then Clint saw the blood. It was seeping through the figure's shirt, low down on the left side, just above the waist. Not a fresh wound, obviously, since there was no hole in the shirt, but bleeding nevertheless.

He crouched down next to the figure and removed the hat from its face.

It was a woman.

EIGHT

The wounded woman did not stir while Clint examined her wound. He pulled her shirt out from her pants and found that the wound had been dressed, but it had obviously been done in haste. He went to his rig for some clean cloth and water. He bathed the wound and saw that, while it was pretty ragged, it was not immediately life-threatening—that is, as long as it did not continue to bleed and did not become infected. But the bullet—which was still inside—would have to be removed.

He dressed the wound cleanly and tried to make the woman more comfortable by putting something beneath her head. There was a gun on the ground next to her right hand. He picked it up and tucked it into his belt, then saw to the fire. Once he had it stoked up to full strength, he put on a pot of coffee and fried up some bacon.

It was after dark before she stirred. If anything, it was probably the smell of the bacon that finally woke the woman up. He was looking at her when her eyes fluttered and then opened.

Under other circumstances she might have been a handsome woman. Her face was haggard and her body slack at the moment, but when she was healthy her face would have been fuller, rounded, and her body straighter. She wasn't tall, and she was full-bodied, a combination that would probably cause her to appear even shorter than she was when she was standing.

Her skin beneath her shirt had been smooth and fair. Her eyes were brown and somewhat bleary at the moment, and her hair was long and brown, though fairly lank right now. He judged her to be about thirty, even making a few years' allowance for her present condition.

"Hello," he said.

She blinked a few times, then looked around for the source of the voice. When she saw him she started and tried to rise, but the pain in her side cut the move short.

He moved to her side with a cup of coffee and said, "Take it easy, or you'll start bleeding again."

"Who're you?" she demanded.

"Just someone who found you in need of help," he said. "Come on, I'll help you to sit up and you can have some coffee."

She reached for the gun which had been on the ground, and came up with a handful of dirt.

"Where's my gun?" she asked.

"I have it."

"Give it back."

"You won't need it now," he said. "Do you want the coffee or not?"

She stared at his face and licked her lips.

"Yes," she said finally, "and some of that bacon too—if it's all right."

She had the presence of mind to be polite. She was a smart one, he decided.

"Let's get you sitting up and you can start on the coffee," he said. "Then I'll get you some bacon and a biscuit."

He helped her to a seated position, leaning back against the tree, and handed her the coffee. While she sipped it he went to the fire, dropped a dry biscuit into the bacon grease until it was soaked, then spooned some bacon and the biscuit into a plate.

"Here," he said, handing her the plate and a fork. She put the coffee cup down on the ground next to her and accepted the food.

"Thanks," she said. She wolfed the food down, and followed it with another cup of coffee. He decided not to question her while she ate, and instead ate with her.

"Could I have some more coffee?" she asked after her second cup.

"Sure," he said. "There's plenty."

"And my gun?"

He looked at her and said, "You're not going to shoot me, are you?"

She scowled and said, "No, but how do I know you're not gonna do something to me?"

"Like what?"

"Like rape me?"

He suppressed a smile, took her gun from his belt, and handed it to her.

"There," he said, "now you're safe."

She checked to make sure the gun was fully loaded, then put it on the ground to her right again.

"You want to tell me your name?" she asked.

"I'll tell you mine if you'll tell me yours."

She hesitated a moment, then shrugged and said, "Well, sure, isn't that the way it always works?"

"Usually," he said. "My name is Clint Adams."

"Mine's Vicky," she said.

"Just Vicky?"

"It'll do for now," she said.

"All right, Vicky," he said. "You want to tell me how you happened to get shot?"

"Look," she said firmly, "I know you helped me, and I'm grateful and all, but that don't entitle you to know my business."

"No, you're right," he said, "it sure doesn't. Come morning I'll just load up my rig and be on my way, leaving you to your business."

"Hey," she said, "you can't—"

"I can't what?" he asked. She was about to protest that he couldn't just leave her there without a horse. "Leave you here without a horse? Somebody already did that, didn't they?"

"No," she said.

"There are tracks all over the place, Vicky," he said. "There *were* other people here, with horses, and they left you here."

"My horse ran off," she said. "Nobody *left* me here without a horse, understand?"

"All right," he said, "I understand. Your horse ran off."

The whites of her eyes looked red, and he thought she might have a fever.

"How long since you were shot?" he asked.

She didn't answer.

He moved to her side and felt her head. She started as he lifted his hand, but suffered his touch when it became obvious that was all he wanted to do.

"You've got a fever," he said. "That wound needs to be tended by a doctor. How long since you were hurt, damn it?"

She hesitated, then said, "A few days . . . maybe."

"All right," he said, "you'd better get some sleep. In the morning I'll put you in my wagon and take you to the nearest town."

"No!" she said. "Not the nearest town."

"You need a doctor."

"I can tell you where to take me."

He frowned at her, then shook his head and said, "Get some sleep. We'll talk about it in the morning."

NINE

In the morning Clint had to wake Vicky. He was tempted to go through her pockets looking for identification, but doubted that he'd be able to do so without waking her. Unlike yesterday, when he had come upon her unconscious, this time she was merely sleeping soundly. He called out to her, and in the end had to shake her awake.

"Wha—" she said, coming awake with a start. She grabbed her gun, and was bringing it up when he took hold of her wrist.

"Easy," he said. "It's only me."

She stared at him for a few moments without recognizing him, then slowly realized who he was. He felt her arm relax, and he released it. She laid the gun back down on the ground next to her.

"Oh," she said.

"Do you always wake up like that?" he asked.

She ignored the question. She looked around her, assuring herself of where she was, and then seemed to sniff the air. "Is that coffee I smell?"

"It is," he said. "I'll get you a cup. After you've had

35

some, and something to eat, why don't we see if you can stand?"

"I can stand," she said a bit belligerently. She started to do so, putting both hands on the ground to push herself up, but she didn't get very far before she decided it was not worth the effort.

"We'll try later," he said, handing her a cup of coffee.

He made bacon and biscuits again and gave her some, which she wolfed down. Her color was good, and her eyes seemed to be clear.

"If you'll sit still I'll check that new dressing I put on you," he said.

She watched him closely as he lifted her shirt just enough to check the dressing. He loosened it on one side so he could look underneath. He didn't see any discoloration of the skin that might indicate an infection, so he reaffixed the dressing and lowered her shirt.

"It looks all right," he said. "The test will be when you stand. If it starts to bleed again we may not be able to travel."

"I'll be able to travel," she said.

He nodded without reply and went to the fire to pour himself a cup of coffee.

When they were both finished he cleaned everything, but left the fire. He'd douse it only when he was sure he could move her.

"Want to try and stand?" he asked.

"Yes."

"Let's go easy," he said.

He moved next to her and put his arms around her to help her up. It did not escape his notice that she made sure to pick up her gun. Slowly, he assisted her to her feet, and then he released her.

"How do you feel?"

"A little weak," she said, and then hastily added, "but all right."

"Good," he said. "Try and take a few steps."

She stook two wobbly steps, then two sturdier ones.

"How's the wound feel?"

"It stings."

"Walk around a little more and then I'll check it to see if it's bleeding."

She walked around the tree a couple of times, then stood still while he checked the wound.

"It looks okay," he said. "You can ride in the back of my wagon. If you need me to stop for any reason, just sing out."

She frowned at him and said, "Where are we going?"

"We have to get you to a doctor," he said.

"I'm not going to Langton," she said.

"Langton?"

"That's the closest town."

"All right, then we won't go to Langton."

"If you're not willing to take me where I want to go," she said, "then you can leave me here. I'll get there on my own."

"How?"

"Walk, if I have to."

"Is it within walking distance?"

She grimaced and said, "Anything is in walking distance if you walk long enough."

He studied her and saw that she was determined to do what she said. One way or another, she would get to where she wanted to go.

"All right."

"All right . . . what?"

"All right, I'll take you where you want to go. Is there a doctor there?"

"There's someone there who can take care of me" was all she'd say.

"All right," he said again, "just tell me where we're going and I'll take you there."

"I'll . . . guide you."

"You can't tell me where it is?"

"I'd rather show you."

"What's the name of this place?"

"That's not important."

"You're an exasperating woman, do you know that?" he asked.

"I don't know what that means."

"Take my word for it," he said. "It's not a compliment. Come on, let's get you into the wagon."

TEN

He helped her into the back of the wagon and tried to make her comfortable. Before she climbed in she stopped to stare in admiration at Duke.

"Why can't I ride him?" she asked.

"Can't," he said.

"Why not?"

"He doesn't let anyone but me ride him."

"That's silly."

"Hey," Clint said, "don't talk to me, talk to him."

She stared at Duke again and said, "He's beautiful."

"Don't let him hear you say that."

She gave Clint a strange look, then climbed into the back of the wagon with his help.

"I don't usually sleep in here," he said. "It's more for work."

She looked around her and saw all sorts of weapons hanging on the wooden walls.

"Do you sell guns?" she asked.

"No," he said, "I repair them."

She looked around again, and saw some knives and even a whip hanging up.

"I also collect a few weapons," he said.

She stared at a cutlass, which had been broken and then sharpened down, and said, "I can see that. Do you know how to use all this stuff?"

"Some of it," he said, nodding. "Some things better than others."

He tossed her a blanket so she could try to get comfortable.

"I don't think anything will fall on you," he said.

"I'll be all right."

"Well, just sing out if you need anything. There's water over here, and some beef jerky if you get hungry."

"I'll eat when you eat," she said.

"Fair enough," he said.

He walked around to the front of the wagon and climbed aboard. He turned to look in at her.

"Which way am I going?"

"Head for Missouri," she said.

"Missouri?"

"Go southeast."

"This would be a lot easier if you would tell me where we're going," he said.

She didn't reply, so he snapped the reins to start the team and headed southeast.

ELEVEN

Clint offered to stop that day for lunch, but Vicky urged him to keep going. They didn't stop then until dusk, when they made camp for the night.

"You can sleep in the wagon tonight if you like," he said at one point.

"Thanks," she said, "but I'd like to get out and stretch my legs some."

He helped her down from the wagon and she tested her legs while he tended to the horses and got the fire going. He put on a pot of coffee, and then opened up a can of beans.

"I'm not that good a cook," he said, as he poured the beans into a pan, "so I usually try to keep everything simple."

"That's fine," she said.

She continued to walk around, keeping her hand pressed to her side. She had her gun tucked into her belt.

The thought had occurred to Clint that she might have been one of the women who robbed the bank in Benbow, but those three women had been headed north, not south. Of course, they could have changed

41

direction, or they could have split up. Whether she was or not, she certainly didn't have any bank money on her. Of course, it was possible that her partners took it, or that it had been on the horse that had run off.

He thought about all of this while he stirred the beans. There was no way to prove she was a bank robber unless she admitted it, and he doubted that she was going to do that. He had no call to accuse her, or to turn her over to the law.

He realized at one point that he was crouched over the fire and she had moved behind him. He listened intently for sounds of trouble, but when he finally turned slowly holding a plate of beans, he saw that she had lowered herself to a seated position on a boulder.

"Thanks," she said as he handed her the food.

He poured a cup of coffee for her and set it down next to her, then spooned out some beans for himself and followed with coffee.

"You haven't asked me any questions all day," she said.

"That doesn't mean I don't have any," he said. "You just don't seem too receptive to them so I decided to stop asking."

She hesitated a moment, then said, "Thanks."

"Just answer me this," he said, and she looked at him sharply.

"What?"

"When I get you to where you want to go," he asked, "am I going to be in trouble?"

"No," she said, scowling at him. "Why should you be? You haven't done me any harm."

"*I* know that," he said.

"No," she said again, "you won't be in any trouble. You'll be able to replace whatever supplies I used up, and be on your way."

It occurred to him that surely wouldn't be the case if she was a bank robber and he was taking her to her hideout, to meet her partners. Still, he'd been operating on instincts for more years than he cared to count, and his instincts told him she was telling the truth.

After they finished eating she stood up and walked around a bit more. He finished cleaning up, checked the stock, and then walked over to her.

"Let me see the wound," he said.

"It's fine," she said.

"Until we reach a real doctor," he said, "*I'm* the doctor and you're the patient. Let me see it."

She sighed, then pulled her shirt up for him to look at it. He thought he felt her flinch when his fingers touched her skin, but it wasn't from pain. She also seemed to be holding her breath.

He replaced the dressing and said, "It looks fine. I guess I'm a better doctor than I thought."

"Lucky for me," she said, tucking her shirt in.

He noticed that her clothing, though more a man's than a woman's, fit her fine. If she was one of the bank robbers who had been dressed in clothing too big for them—to hide the fact that they were women—then she had since changed clothes. That would explain why there was no bullet hole in her shirt. She would have discarded the clothing she'd worn while wounded.

"You've got that look on your face," she said.

"What look?"

"Like you're thinking of a lot of questions."

"I am," he said, "but I won't ask them. Why don't we turn in?"

"Sure," she said, "but you can have the wagon."

"I hardly ever sleep in the wagon," he said. "It's yours if you want it. If you don't, I'll still be sleeping outside."

"All right," she said. "I'll take the wagon."

He helped her up into the wagon and told her, "Sleep well. If you need me, just holler out."

"Thanks," she said. For a moment a soft look came over her face, as if she were letting down the defenses she'd had up since they'd met. "Thanks for everything."

"You're welcome," he said. "Good night."

"Night."

He checked the animals one more time before rolling himself up in his blanket, putting his head on his saddle, and going to sleep.

TWELVE

Clint woke during the night, unsure of what it was that had awakened him. Slowly, he put his hand on his gun, which was right next to his head in his holster. With the other hand he made sure the blanket was free, so that he wouldn't become tangled in it when he made his move.

Abruptly, he turned and leveled the gun—at Vicky, who was sitting by the fire, drinking coffee. She started, spilling the coffee into the fire, where it quickly became steam, clouding the air between them.

"Jesus!" she said.

"I'm sorry," he said, lowering the gun. "I didn't know it was you."

"Who did you think it was?" she asked.

He tossed off the blanket, holstered the gun, and joined her at the fire. He picked up the coffeepot and poured her another cup, and then one for himself. He hadn't answered her question.

"Are you always this jumpy?" she asked.

"Now you're asking questions?"

She looked away and said, "Sorry."

"It's okay," he said. "I don't have anything to hide."

"And I do?" she asked quickly.

"That's not what I meant," he said.

The tension between them hung in the air for a few moments, and then he felt it disappear.

"Maybe I do have something to hide," she said, "but I'm not ready to talk about it . . . yet."

"That's fine," he said. "Whenever you're ready, I'm here . . . and if you're *not* ready, that's fine too. It's really none of my business."

"I don't mean to treat you badly," she said. "I mean, you've done a lot for me—you're *doing* a lot for me."

"Vicky—"

"Would you check my wound again?" she asked suddenly. "It . . . itches."

"That means it's healing . . . but I'll check it."

He moved to her side of the fire and she turned to face him. He was aware of something between them. Something in their relationship had changed. Since *he* had done nothing different, he had to assume it was on her part.

"Couldn't sleep?" he asked as she lifted her shirt.

"No," she said.

Was she lifting her shirt higher than before? Higher than was necessary?

"Because of the wound?"

She hesitated, then said, "No." When his fingertips touched her she caught her breath. Again, he did not think it was from pain.

"The wound looks fine," he said.

"Look . . . closer . . ." she said.

"Vicky . . ."

She continued to lift her shirt, bunching it as she went, and suddenly her breasts were bare. Her nipples were distended, and she was breathing heavily.

"Vicky . . ."

"Clint," she said, "it's been a long time . . . when you touch me I . . ."

He touched her again, his fingertips on her abdomen, and then higher. He had one of her nipples in his fingers, squeezing it, and then he moved the other hand onto her. Hc was holding both of her breasts, kneading them, and then he leaned forward to run his mouth over them.

"Oh, God," she said, and lifted the shirt over her head without unbuttoning it. She dropped to the ground and put her hands on his shoulders as he kissed and licked her full breasts.

"Oh . . . good . . ." she said.

"We have to be careful . . ." he said. "Your wound . . . lie back . . ." he said. And then, "Wait . . ."

He retrieved his blanket and put it on the ground behind her, then helped her lie back on it. Gently, he pulled off her boots, then undid her trousers and eased them down her legs. He could smell her then, thc sharp girl odor that said she was ready. He removed her underwear, one hand beneath her, lifting her, and then he kept her butt lifted off the ground and settled between her legs with his face. When his tongue touched her she gasped audibly and her body rippled with pleasure. It had been a long time for her, that much was clear. She spasmed several more times while he licked her, until she was whimpering and reaching for him . . .

He raised himself over her, lowered his trousers and underwear, and without removing a stitch of clothing himself, carefully entered her without putting pressure on her. He held himself above her with a hand on either side, and began to move in her. She reached for him to pull him down to her, but he resisted. If he allowed his weight to rest on her she would begin to bleed for sure.

He continued working in and out of her that way until she cried out and shuddered, and then he exploded inside her . . .

He covered her afterward and sat next to her while she recovered her breath, and her senses.

"God," she said, breathlessly, "it had been so long . . . and every time you touched me . . ."

He put his hand on her face and she turned her head and took his thumb into her mouth. She started to suck it, and he felt the tingling right down to his groin.

"Vicky," he said, easing his thumb out of her mouth, "we'd better go easy . . ."

"I don't want to go easy," she said fiercely. He was surprised by the tears that glistened in her eyes.

"We have to," he said. "We don't want you to start bleeding again."

Having said that he took the time to check her wound again. Luckily, their activity had not started it bleeding again.

"We were lucky," he said.

"I was lucky," she said. "Lucky that it was you who found me."

He decided not to ask who could have found her who would have made her unlucky. Maybe, after what they had just been through together, she'd soon be giving him answers to his questions without his even having to ask them.

He rearranged his own clothing, and then helped her to get dressed. He then lowered her to the blanket again when she said she didn't want to go into the wagon.

"I'd like to stay here by the fire," she said, "with you . . . if that's all right."

He lay down with her there and they slept that way together . . .

THIRTEEN

When they woke the next morning Clint sensed Vicky's embarrassment. They had breakfast without saying much to each other, and then while Clint was breaking camp Vicky walked away, as if she wanted to be alone. She came back as he was kicking dirt onto the remnants of the fire.

"We have to talk before we go on," she said.

"All right."

"I guess you know how . . . awkward I feel after last night."

"Last night was fine, Vicky," he said. "There's nothing to feel awkward about. I don't expect anything from you, and I don't think you expect anything from me."

"Clint," she said, "when we get closer to where . . . we're going, it might be wise for me to go on alone, on foot."

"Why is that?"

"Well . . . I wasn't completely honest with you when I said you would be safe when we got there," she said. "I mean, I think I can keep you safe, but I don't know if I can guarantee it."

"You mean someone might want to kill me?"

"There's an awful lot . . . you don't know."

"I know that," he said.

"Well, you might not *want* to know," she said. "And I might want to tell you, but I can't. Not without being . . . disloyal to some other people."

"I wouldn't want you to do that, Vicky," he said. "Loyalty is very important."

"I know," she said. "We all feel that way." She bit her lip immediately following that statement, as if by making it she had let something slip. All he could infer from it was that there were quite a few other people involved.

"Well," he said, "I'll leave it up to you then."

"To me?"

"Yes," he said. "When we reach that certain point, you decide if you want to go on without me, or if you want me to come along. I'll abide by your decision."

"You'll . . . trust me?"

"Why not?" he asked. "Didn't you just tell me how trustworthy you are?"

"Well, yes, but . . . you don't know me."

"I know you better than I did," he said, and she blushed. "That's something."

"That's a lot," she said, unable to meet his eyes.

"Vicky," he said, moving to her and taking her by the shoulders. She looked up at him and he said, "I trust you not to let any harm come to me."

She stared at him for a moment. Then she hugged him, pressing her head to his chest, and said, "Oh, I won't, I *swear* I won't, Clint."

"Well, okay then," he said, holding her off at arm's length. "Maybe we should get started then."

"Yes," she said.

He stowed the gear back in the wagon and hooked up the team. Instead of putting the saddle in the wagon, though, he decided to go ahead and saddle Duke, just in case.

Maybe he didn't trust her as much as he said he did.

They traveled once again without stopping for lunch. Instead, they ate beef jerky while they continued on. Vicky felt well enough to climb up and sit next to him, and they ate together, washing the dried beef down with water.

Along about midday Clint saw a dust cloud up ahead, and stopped.

"What is it?" Vicky asked.

"Somebody's coming this way," he said. "Looks like a few riders."

"Where?"

"Up ahead."

She squinted and said, "I don't see anything."

"See all that dust? It's being kicked up by a few riders."

"Can we go around them?" she asked. He felt her body go tense.

"I take it it's not going to be anyone you know?" he asked.

"I doubt it."

"But it's somebody you'd rather not see?"

She looked at him and said, "More than likely."

"Well," he said, rubbing his jaw, "we can't go around them. They're moving too fast and we're going too slow. They'll see us anyway."

"Well, then, I'll get in the back," she said, and started to do that.

"That's not a good idea," he said, putting his hand on her to stop her.

"Why not?"

"Because if they decide to search the wagon I may not be able to stop them. Then, if they find you hiding back there, it won't look good for you."

"But if I stay up here with you they'll see me."

"I don't know who or what they're looking for," he said, "and you probably do. Would they be looking for a man and a woman traveling together?"

"No, they wouldn't."

"Well, then," he said, "that's what we'll let them see."

FOURTEEN

Clint continued on at a leisurely pace, and before long the riders came into view. There were about eight of them, and they were riding hard. When they spotted the wagon they slowed, and seemed to be trying to decide what to do. Eventually, they came on again, riding straight for Clint and Vicky.

"Just stay quiet," he said. "If you talk, just go along with whatever I say."

"Right."

As the riders approached the one in the lead waved, a wave that said, "Stop," and not, "Hello."

Clint reined in the team and waited for the riders to reach them. The man riding in the lead was wearing a badge. The group had all the looks of a posse.

"Good afternoon," Clint called out. "What can we do for you gents? If you need water we can probably spare you some."

"We have enough water, but thanks for the offer," the man said. "I'm Sheriff Rhodes, from Langton. This here is a duly deputized posse."

"I see," Clint said. "Who is it you're looking for, Sheriff?"

"Three bank robbers," he said. "They held up our bank and got away with about six thousand dollars."

"When did that happen?"

"About five days ago," the sheriff said.

"And you're still looking?"

"Can't rightly stop, Mr. . . . "

"Adams," Clint said, leaving out his first name. "This is my wife."

"Ma'am," the sheriff said, touching the brim of his hat in gentlemanly fashion. "Well, Mr. Adams, where are you coming from?"

"From Benbow way actually."

"You didn't happen to come across three riders along the way, did you?" the sheriff asked. "Maybe riding their mounts hard?"

"Can't say as we did," Clint said. He looked at Vicky and said, "Did you notice anything, honey?"

"No, dear," she said. She seemed to be having trouble looking directly at the sheriff. Clint hoped the man wouldn't notice.

"One or more of them may be wounded," the sheriff said. "We shot it out with them pretty fierce."

"I hope no one in town was hurt," Clint said.

"No, we got off with no casualties, thank the Lord, but they did get away with our money."

"Well, we're sorry we couldn't help you," Clint said. "Oh, by the way, I repair guns for a living. If any of you gents have need of my services at the moment I'd be glad to stop awhile and oblige."

The sheriff turned and looked at his men, all of whom shook their heads.

"No, our weapons are in working order, Mr. Adams. Thanks just the same. We better be moving on."

"I wish you luck."

"Thanks," the sheriff said. He touched his hat again and said, "Ma'am."

Vicky looked at him, nodded, and then looked away again.

"Let's go, men."

The posse split in two and rode around the wagon. Clint knew that they were probably trying to get a look inside without asking to. That was fine by him. They wouldn't see anything.

As they rode by he heard one man comment to another, "Fine-lookin' woman."

Clint doubted that Vicky had heard the compliment. He snapped the reins and started the team moving at a leisurely pace.

Next to him Vicky sat quietly, her shoulders hunched. He guessed she was waiting for him to ask her some questions. He decided he wouldn't. He'd just have to wait and see if she wanted to tell him anything, and if so, how much.

He still had no way of knowing for sure that she *was* one of the bank robbers, but it seemed more than likely now that if she *was* a bank robber, she was one of the ones who had held up the bank in the town of Langton, and not the one in Benbow. *That* job had to have been pulled by a different trio of robbers. He was pleased, though, that no one in Langton had been hurt, or killed. Had that been the case, he would have been faced with the very difficult decision of whether or not to turn her over to the sheriff from Langton for questioning.

Two bank robberies that close together, within days of each other? That was certainly too much of a coincidence for a man who didn't *believe* in coincidence to begin with—especially if both robberies were committed by a trio of women.

And what would he find when he and Vicky finally reached their destination? That is, if she took him all the way there with her. A whole camp filled with female bank robbers?

Wouldn't that be interesting?

FIFTEEN

The town of Freedom was literally *on* the border between Kansas and Missouri. That meant that half the town was in Kansas and the other half was in Missouri. As far as the law went, though, the inhabitants of the town made their own.

If the town had a mayor, it was Nancy Peeples.

If it had a sheriff, that was Lisa Ford.

On the "town council" sat Oriana Hardy, Donna Murray, Jan Grape, Kate Dougherty, and Barbara Petty.

All of the positions of authority were held by women. All of the businesses were owned by women. In point of fact, the entire town was populated by women.

There were no men.

By any standards Freedom was a small town. The total population was no more than twenty to twenty-five at any one time. There were more uninhabited buildings than there were inhabited buildings, but that was okay. When Freedom was first founded by the five women who served on the council, plus Nancy Peeples and Lisa Ford, *they* had been the only ones who lived there. As time went by, they had been able to convince

other women to come and join them in their new man-
less Utopia.

At the present time there were twenty-four women
living in Freedom. When Vicky Tanner arrived, they
would be back up to twenty-five.

If Vicky Tanner arrived . . .

"You never should have left her," Lisa Ford said.

Gloria Estes looked down at the floor and shuffled her
feet. She had been the leader of the three women who
went to Langton. It had been her decision to leave the
wounded Vicky behind, so that she and Betty Baker
could get the money back to Freedom.

"Never mind that," Nancy Peeples said. "Gloria, you
can leave."

Nancy Peeples was standing. Seated around the table
were the five members of the town council: Ori, Jan,
Donna, Kate, and Barbara. Standing in the corner with
her arms folded across her chest was Lisa Ford.

"What about the others?" Nancy asked Lisa.

"They're back," she said. "No problem."

The "others" were Jody Watts, Paula Simon, and
Carly Taylor, the three women who had held up the
bank at Benbow.

Now that Gloria Estes had left the room, the only ones
remaining were the seven "founders" of Freedom.

"Do we know how bad Vicky's wound was?"
Kate Dougherty asked. She was perhaps the prettiest
of the women in the room, but she was also the
smallest. Barely five feet tall, she had long blond
hair and a delicately boned face. She was in her late
thirties.

"According to Gloria," Lisa Ford said, touching her
side, "she was hit here. It didn't appear to be serious,

but she was bleeding. The only way to stop the bleeding was to let her rest."

"Which they couldn't do while they were being chased by a posse," Nancy said.

"Right," Lisa said.

Lisa Ford was a statuesque blonde in her mid-thirties, possibly the most classically lovely of the women. She had blond hair, worn long like Kate Dougherty's, but there the similarity between the two women ended. Lisa was almost a foot taller than Kate.

Nancy Peeples was about five-seven, with brown hair cut to frame her face. She had a rangy, athletic build that many of the other women admired and envied. She was in her early thirties.

The women in the room ranged in age from thirty to early fifties. Donna Murray and Barbara Petty were forty-six and forty-eight respectively, and yet both women were what could be described as "handsome." Both were dark-haired and fair-complected, Murray shorter and more full-bodied, Petty taller and more slender.

Ori Hardy was what most men would describe as a "fine figure of a woman." She stood about five-foot-eight or so, and was built along very solid lines. One might even have called her "Rubenesque."

Jan Grape was the oldest woman in the room. In her early fifties, she had recently lost a lot of weight—by choice—and was now a perfect example of what a woman her age should look like. She had short brown hair and a pronounced Texas twang.

All of the women in the room—indeed, all of the women in the town—felt they had been wronged at one time or another in their lives by men. It was for that reason that the first seven women had founded Freedom, and why the others had come to live there.

Unfortunately, it took money to keep a town running, and it soon became apparent to "the Seven"—as the townspeople had come to call them—that without a thriving populace, there was only one way for them to get the money they needed.

Because the town was virtually split between two states, "the Seven" made sure that the women who pulled the robberies in Missouri lived on the Kansas side, and the women who did the robberies in Kansas lived on the Missouri side.

At the moment the Seven were concerned not only that one of their number was missing and possibly dead, but also that she might have been captured.

"If the law caught her, would she talk?" Ori Hardy asked.

"Who knows Vicky well enough to answer that?" Nancy asked.

"I do," Donna Murray said. "I sponsored her."

Before a new woman could be welcomed to live in Freedom, she had to be sponsored by someone already living there.

"Well?" Lisa Ford asked.

"I don't think she would," Donna said.

"You don't think?" Nancy asked.

Donna shrugged helplessly and said, "There's no way I can be sure, but I *feel* that she would not."

"Maybe someone should go and look for her," Barbara Petty suggested.

"That's a possibility," Nancy said.

"No," Lisa Ford said.

"Why not?"

"Because there are two Kansas posses out looking for bank robbers."

"They may not know they're looking for women," Kate Dougherty said.

"And then again they might," Lisa said. "We've got to let the heat die down before we start traipsing all over the countryside looking for somebody who was careless enough to get herself shot."

"How about a little more compassion, Lisa?" Donna Murray said.

"It might not have been a good idea to pull two robberies in the same area so close together," Jan Grape said, interrupting them before an argument could get started.

The statement hung in the air. The Seven had been split on this issue. Jan Grape, Donna Murray, and Barbara Petty had been against the idea, while Kate Dougherty, Ori Hardy, and Lisa Ford had been in favor. The deciding vote had been cast by Nancy Peeples. It was a vote she had agonized over. The town needed money, and the women she had sent out to scout for Missouri banks had not yet returned at that time. She had decided to go ahead and try it. She still wasn't convinced it had been the *wrong* thing to do, but even so . . .

"Maybe it wasn't a good idea," Nancy said, "but what's done is done."

"So what's to be done about Vicky?" Donna Murray asked. "We can't just leave her out there."

"We'll have to give her some time to get back on her own," Lisa Ford said.

"Today's Wednesday," Nancy said. "We'll give her to the end of the week. If she's not back by then someone can go look for her."

"Who?" Lisa asked.

Nancy looked at Lisa, and then the others, and said, "It'll have to be a volunteer."

They all looked around the room, wondering who that volunteer would be.

SIXTEEN

"Stop here," Vicky said.

Clint brought the team to a stop without question.

"My name is Vicky Tanner," she said.

"Hello, Vicky Tanner."

She smiled wanly, and then said, "Maybe I should go on from here on my own."

"On foot?"

"Yes."

"How far would you have to walk?"

"A few miles," she said.

"That means you might not make it by dark," he said.

"I know."

"You also might be too weak to make it on foot at all," he pointed out.

"I'll rest when I get tired."

"I don't think so."

"Clint—"

"I'll take you all the way in, Vicky," he said.

She hesitated, and then said, "Well, then, I guess you should know what you're getting yourself in for."

"Can we drive while you tell me?"

"Yes."

So they continued on, and Vicky told Clint all about the town called Freedom.

"So *all* of the women in town feel they've been wronged by men?" he asked afterward.

"That's right."

"Even you?"

"Oh, yes," she said. "I thought that all men were the same . . . but I'm starting to have second thoughts about that now."

"I'll take that as a compliment," he said.

"I guess I'm not even sure now if I *belong* in Freedom," she said.

"Can I ask a question?"

"Sure."

"Once you become a citizen of Freedom," he asked, "can you get out?"

There was a long pause and then Vicky said slowly, "I don't think anybody's ever asked that question before."

They both pondered that question until they came within sight of Freedom.

"It's not a very big town," she said almost apologetically, "and we don't even have enough people to fill it."

"How many people—er, women—live there?" Clint asked her.

"Twenty-five, I think."

"Do you have officials—I mean a sheriff, and a mayor, and all of that?"

"We have the Seven."

"The Seven?" he asked. "What's that?"

"The seven women who founded the town," she said. "They make up the town council, and one is the sheriff and one the mayor—unofficially, of course. I mean,

Lisa's the sheriff, but she doesn't wear a badge or anything."

"Lisa?"

"Lisa Ford," Vicky said. "She and Nancy—Nancy Peeples—actually run the whole show. I mean, I think they were the first two to come up with the idea for Freedom."

"I see."

"Clint," she said, putting her hand on his arm, "you can still let me off and leave."

"Nah," he said, "I've come this far, I'd like to go all the way."

She squeezed his arm and silently hoped that she *would* be able to keep him safe.

"Shall we go in?" he asked.

"I guess so," she said.

SEVENTEEN

Lisa Ford and Kate Dougherty made an odd-looking couple walking down the street. Both blond, both lovely, but Lisa almost a foot taller than the smaller woman. Nevertheless, a man would have a rough time choosing between the two.

They had just left the meeting of the Seven and were on their way to Lisa's office. They suspended any con-versation until they were behind closed doors in the "sheriff's office."

"What do you think?" Kate asked.

"I think Nancy might be starting to go soft," Lisa said.

Even though the Seven had founded Freedom, it had been Nancy and Lisa who'd come up with the *idea* of a town like Freedom, a town where a woman would not have to depend on a man for anything. But even though Nancy and Lisa were considered the founding "mothers," Lisa had a closer relationship with Kate Dougherty, who was her unofficial deputy—and what other kind of deputy would an "unofficial" sheriff have?

"She voted with us when we were trying to decide whether or not to pull two jobs at the same time in Kansas," Kate reminded Lisa.

"I know that," Lisa said, "but it was a tentative vote at best."

Lisa removed her gunbelt and placed it in the bottom drawer of her desk. She was the only woman in Freedom who wore a gun in town, but then again she was the only woman who knew how to use a pistol well. There were several others who could use a rifle—Nancy, and Kate Dougherty—but Lisa was the only one who was accurate with a handgun—and she was *extremely* accurate. Many of the women in town found her ability with a gun to be uncanny.

Lisa sat behind the desk while Kate poured two cups of coffee from the pot that was always going on the potbellied stove in the corner.

"Here," Kate said. She set Lisa's cup down on the desk, and seated herself across from her friend.

"I mean," Lisa said, continuing as if there had been no pause in the conversation, "Nancy's willing to send someone out to look for Vicky at the end of the week. As far as I'm concerned, Vicky can fend for herself. I mean, that's what this whole town is about, isn't it?"

"I thought so," Kate said.

"I mean, a few *months* ago she never would have even considered it," Lisa said. In point of fact, Freedom had only been in existence for six months.

"What are you saying?" Kate asked.

"I'm saying that maybe Nancy shouldn't be mayor anymore."

"And who should? You?"

"Me?" Lisa said. "No, not me. I like the job I have now. No, Kate, I was thinking about you."

"Me?" Kate said. "Why me?"

"Because you and I think alike," Lisa said. "We work well together."

"That's true enough," Kate said. "She'd have to be voted out, though."

"I know."

"Who would vote with us?"

"Ori would vote with us," Lisa said. "That means we'd only have to win over Donna, Jan, or Barbara."

"Donna's out," Kate said. "She brought Vicky in, and she'll probably volunteer to go out and look for her."

"Okay, that leaves Barbara and Jan," Lisa said. "I tell you what. You talk to Barbara, and I'll talk to Jan—and let's try not to look like we're trying to win them over or anything. Let's just sound them out and see what happens, okay?"

"Sure, Lisa," Kate said.

"I've got a lot of backing in town," Lisa said. "Even if it were put to a total vote of everyone in town, I think they'd go with me."

"Nancy has a lot of friends, Lisa," Kate warned.

"I know," Lisa said. "That's why we have to be careful about this. Don't say anything to anyone until we're ready to make our move."

"I understand."

"I know you do, Kate," Lisa said. "That's why we'll make a good team and run Freedom the way it *should* be run, because *we* understand each other."

Of course, it didn't occur to either woman at that point that Nancy Peeples and Lisa Ford had at one time thought very much alike. Over the course of the past six months—more specifically, the past *three* months—Lisa Ford's thinking had changed dramatically.

Once, she and Nancy had agreed that the stealing would be kept to a minimum. They would only steal what they needed to keep the town going. Now, Lisa

Ford had started to think that the more they could get away with, the better, and Nancy obviously didn't feel that way.

That meant that to get her way Lisa was going to have to take more control over Freedom, and *that* meant voting Nancy Peeples out.

And if that didn't work, there were others methods of getting her out of the way.

After the meeting of the Seven broke up, everyone left but Nancy Peeples and Donna Murray. Donna remained seated and Nancy sat across the table from her.

"I'll go out and look for Vicky at the end of the week," Donna said to Nancy.

"I know you will, Donna," Nancy said. "Maybe you can get someone else to volunteer to go with you."

"Lisa won't like that," Donna said.

Nancy sighed and said, "Yes, I know that."

"You and Lisa seem to be drifting further apart, Nancy," Donna said. "Others have noticed it too."

"She's changed, Donna," Nancy said. "I don't know how or when exactly, but she's changed."

"Maybe—" Donna started, but she stopped when the door opened suddenly and a girl named Nia came running in. At seventeen, Nia was the youngest woman in Freedom, the closest thing to a child the town had.

"Nancy, I think you better come outside," Nia said anxiously.

"What's wrong, Nia?"

"Vicky's back," Nia said.

Nancy and Donna exchanged glances, and Donna said to Nia, "That's good."

"You might not think so when you come outside," Nia said.

"Why not?" Nancy asked. "Come on, Nia, what's going on?"

"She's back," Nia said, "and she's brought a man with her."

EIGHTEEN

As Clint drove the rig down the center of the street women began coming out of buildings, staring at him and Vicky Tanner.

"I guess it's been a while since they've seen a man," he said.

"In Freedom anyway," Vicky said. "Over there, in front of the town hall. That's Nancy Peeples."

Clint saw an athletically built woman with short brown hair standing with a full-bodied, dark-haired woman who was a bit older than Nancy.

"Who's the other woman?"

"That's Donna Murray," Vicky said. "She sponsored me so I could come and live in Freedom. What I've done will probably get us both kicked out."

Clint didn't know if she meant getting shot, or bringing him into town.

He stopped the rig directly in front of the town hall. Nancy Peeples stood staring at him with her hands on her hips. Donna Murray, on the other hand, was staring questioningly at Vicky.

Clint dropped down and walked around the rig to help Vicky down. By now, if all of the women of Freedom weren't on the street, there were damned few who weren't.

Clint heard the sound of heavy footsteps coming down the boardwalk, and saw a tall, blond woman striding purposefully towards them. She was wearing a gun on her hip. He assumed that this was Lisa Ford, Freedom's "unofficial" sheriff. Behind her a smaller woman, also blond, trotted to keep up with her. She was carrying a rifle.

"Vicky," Nancy said, "I'm glad to see you back."

"Thanks, Nancy."

"Are you all right?"

"I'm fine," she said.

"She's not fine," Clint said. "She still has a bullet inside of her, and it should be removed. Do you have someone who can do that?"

"Nia?" Nancy called.

"Yes, Nancy?" the young girl answered. She had been staring at Clint with unabashed curiosity.

"Take Vicky over to your mother's," Nancy said.

"Nancy, we should talk first," Vicky said. "This is Clint Adams. He probably saved my life, and—"

"We'll talk, Vicky," Nancy said, "but after you've been taken care of. Nia, have someone go with you."

"Yes, Nancy."

"I'll go with her," Donna Murray said.

"Fine," Nancy said.

"Meanwhile," Lisa Ford said, taking her gun from her holster and pointing it at Clint, "I'll take the gentleman over to the jail."

"No!" Vicky said. "Nancy!"

Nancy looked at Vicky, and then at Clint.

"It might be best, Vicky," Nancy finally said. "At least until we can talk." She looked pointedly at Clint and said, "Your friend will cooperate, won't he?"

Vicky put her hand on Clint's arm.

"It's all right, Vicky," Clint said. He looked at Nancy and said, "Of course I'll cooperate. After all, I'm a guest in your town."

"That's right," Nancy said. "You are."

"Let me have your gun," Lisa said.

Clint looked at Lisa. If her face hadn't been so severely set she would have been one of the most beautiful women he had ever seen.

He removed his gun from his holster and held it out.

"Take it, Kate," Lisa said.

The smaller blonde stepped forward and took the gun. Her blue eyes were fixed on Clint's face.

"Vicky, go on and get taken care of," Nancy said. "Your friend, Mr. Adams, will be fine."

Donna Murray stepped into the street and put her hand on Vicky's arm. As Vicky walked away with her Clint heard the young girl, Nia, ask her, "Did it hurt to get shot, Vick?"

"Nia," Donna said, "be quiet."

"I was just asking . . ."

"Mr. Adams, if you'll go with our sheriff, Lisa Ford," Nancy said, "we can talk later, after we've had a chance to talk with Vicky."

"Sure," Clint said. "Will someone take care of my horses and my rig?"

"We'll look after them," Nancy assured him.

Clint looked at Lisa Ford and said, "Lead the way, Sheriff."

"Walk ahead of me, mister," Lisa said, gesturing with her gun.

"Lisa," Nancy said, "I don't think you'll need the gun."

Lisa turned and said to Nancy, "Well, I do," and then marched Clint down to the jail with Kate trailing behind them.

Nancy stared after Donna and Nia as they walked Vicky to Nia's mother's place. Nia's mother, Margaret Colin, was not a doctor, but a nurse. She was, however, the closest thing they had to a doctor.

Nancy stared also after Lisa and Kate, who were leading Vicky's friend—at least, her benefactor—to the jail.

If Nancy was any judge, something more had happened between the man Clint Adams and Vicky other than his just saving her life.

She had a feeling that things were going to get even more complicated in the town of Freedom.

NINETEEN

Clint walked meekly to the jail, and allowed Lisa Ford to lock him in a cell. She didn't say anything to him, but she gave him a little push into the cell, and then glared at him while she locked the door. She went back into the office and dropped the keys on the desk.

"Keep an eye on him," she said to Kate.

"He can't go anywhere, Lisa."

"Just watch him," Lisa said. "I'll be back in a little while."

"Sure."

After Lisa left, Kate walked in the back to take a better look at Clint.

"Hello," Clint said.

"Hi."

"What's your name?"

"Kate," the little blonde said, "Kate Dougherty."

"Hi, Kate," he said, "I'm Clint."

"You saved Vicky's life, huh?"

"Well, I found her and did what I could for her wound," he said. "Anyone else would have done the same."

"Maybe."

"Of course," he said, looking around the cell, "this isn't exactly the kind of thanks I expected."

"Oh," Kate said, "you'll be out of here in no time."

"I hope so," Clint said.

Actually, Clint was starting to wonder if this had been such a good idea. If these women robbed banks and such for a living, what were the chances that they would just let him leave town? All along he hadn't really taken the whole thing seriously, but now that he was locked in a cell he was starting to wonder.

He just *might* have made an error in judgment here.

Lisa Ford walked to Margaret Colin's office and entered without knocking. Both Donna Murray and Nia Colin were still there, in the waiting room.

"Where's Vicky?" Lisa demanded.

"Inside," Donna said.

"Mother's working on her," Nia said.

"I have to talk to her," Lisa said, and started towards the door to the examination room. She had taken only two steps when Donna Murray stepped in front of her.

"You can't go in there."

"Get out of my way, Donna."

"No," Donna said. "You can talk to Vicky after Margaret has taken care of her."

"I have to talk to her *now*," Lisa said. "What does she mean by bringing a man here?"

"I don't know," Donna said, "but she can explain after she's recovered."

"Out of my way, Donna!" Lisa shouted.

"You can't bully me, Lisa!" Donna shouted back.

Abruptly the other door opened and Margaret Colin stepped out. She was about thirty-eight, tall, with short-cropped dark hair.

"What the hell is going on out here?" she demanded.

"I have to talk to Vicky," Lisa said, glaring at Donna.

"Tomorrow," Margaret said.

Lisa looked away from Donna directly at Margaret.

"I have to talk to her *now*, Maggie."

"And I said tomorrow, Lisa," Margaret said. "I've just taken a bullet out of her and she's resting."

"She can rest while I talk to her."

"Damn it, Lisa," Margaret snapped, "stop trying to throw your weight around. Vicky's in my care and I'll let you know when you can talk to her."

At that moment the outer door opened and Nancy Peeples walked in. She took one look at the situation and surmised what was going on.

"Lisa," she said, wearily, "can't you wait to talk to poor Vicky?"

"Poor Vicky," Lisa said, "has jeopardized us all by bringing that . . . that . . . man here."

"Maybe she has," Nancy said, "and maybe she hasn't. We'll talk to her about it when Margaret says she's well enough to talk."

"Tomorrow," Margaret said.

"All right," Nancy said, "tomorrow."

Lisa looked around the room, and finding herself hopelessly outnumbered, stormed out.

"What's going on with her, Nancy?" Margaret asked.

"I've been asking myself the same question," Nancy said. "Margaret, how's Vicky?"

"She's be all right," Margaret said. "Whoever that man is, he did a fine job on her. He kept her from bleeding to death, and also kept the wound clean and free of infection. He most likely saved her life."

Nancy frowned. That was going to make matters even more complicated.

"Where is he anyway?" Margaret asked.

"He's in jail," Nia said.

"In jail? My God, Nancy, he saved Vicky's life, for Chrissake."

"I know," Nancy said, "I know. Lisa was just being careful, Maggie."

"If you ask me," Donna said, "Lisa's been getting a little too careful, lately."

"She just believes that you can't be *too* careful," Nancy said.

"Nancy," Donna said. "I think lately this whole thing has been getting out of hand."

"Let's not talk about that here, Donna," Nancy said. She didn't want Donna forgetting that Margaret and her daughter were not part of the Seven. Donna was afraid that the Seven might have lately started to think of themselves as some sort of exalted group, like the twelve Apostles.

"You've got to get that man out of jail," Margaret said.

"I know, I know," Nancy said. "I'll take care of it, Margaret."

"I hope so."

"What about Vicky, Margaret?"

"I'll keep her here a while, and then she can go home—but she's going to have to stay in bed for a while."

"Donna?" Nancy said.

"I'll take her home, Nancy."

"All right," Nancy said. "I better go and talk to Lisa."

"Good luck," Margaret said.

"I'll probably need it . . ."

TWENTY

"So how long do you figure to keep me in here?" Clint asked Kate.

"I guess that'd be up to Lisa."

"Oh," Clint said. "If it's up to her I guess I'll be in here forever."

"She's not that bad," Kate said.

"She looked at me like she hated me."

"Lisa hates all men," Kate said.

"Is that right?" Clint said. "What about you? Do you hate all men?"

Kate smiled and said, "Men have their uses."

"A woman as beautiful as you, you'd know that, huh?" he asked.

Unconsciously, Kate touched her hair. It had been a long time since a man had told her she was beautiful. Of course, she had been in Freedom a long time. She decided that she liked it. She moved closer to the cell.

"So tell me, why did you stop to help Vicky?" she asked.

"Because she needed help."

"That's all?"

"What other reason would there be?"

"I don't know," Kate said, "I'm asking you."

"I saw someone who needed help," he said. "I would have done the same for anyone."

"And then you brought her all the way here?"

"She needed a ride," he said. "I couldn't let her walk here. She never would have made it."

Kate opened her mouth to say something else, but she heard someone come into the office and backed away from the bars quickly.

"Lisa?"

"No," a voice said, "it's Nancy."

Nancy Peeples appeared in the doorway. "Lisa's still not here, I take it?"

"She went to talk to Vicky, I think," Kate said.

"I know," Nancy said. "I saw her over there. Margaret said Vicky can't talk until tomorrow."

"Is she all right?" Clint asked.

"Yes, she's fine," Nancy said, "thanks to you. Margaret—she's our nurse—said that you probably saved her life."

"I'm glad to hear it," Clint said.

"Kate," Nancy said, "where are the keys to the cell?"

"Uh, they're on the desk, Nancy, but I can't let him out. Lisa said—"

"You're not letting him out," Nancy said. "I am."

"Nancy," Kate said, going into the office after Nancy, who was taking the keys off the desk. "Lisa's gonna be real mad."

"You tell Lisa to come and talk to me," Nancy said. "This man saved Vicky's life, and he deserves better than to be in here."

Nancy walked to the cell door and unlocked it. "You can come out, Mr. Adams."

"Thank you, Miss . . . "

"Mrs. Peeples."

"Thank you, Mrs. Peeples," he said, stepping outside.

"Give him his gun, Kate."

"Nancy . . . "

"Just give it to him," Nancy said impatiently.

Kate still had Clint's gun in her belt, and she took it out and gave it to him now.

"Thank you," he said.

"You're probably hungry," Nancy said.

"I could use some cleaning up too," he said.

"I'll take you to the hotel," Nancy said. "You can get a bath there. Afterwards, we'll get you something to eat."

"I appreciate it, Mrs. Peeples."

"Come on," Nancy said. "I'll see you later, Kate."

"Bye, Kate," Clint said.

"Bye," Kate said somewhat helplessly.

Outside, Clint followed Nancy Peeples down the street to the hotel. Inside, behind the desk, a woman watched them enter.

"Belle," Nancy said, "this is Mr. Adams. Mr. Adams, this is Belle Walker. She runs the hotel for us."

"Pleased to meet you," Belle said, eyeing Clint up and down with obvious pleasure.

Belle was an overweight women in her forties with rosy cheeks and pudgy hands. At that moment she wished she had her pudgy hands all over Clint Adams.

"Belle," Nancy said, her tone stern, "give Mr. Adams a room and have a bath drawn for him."

"Sure, Nancy."

"I'll come back for you in half an hour, Mr. Adams," Nancy said. "Belle will take good care of you—won't you, Belle?"

"I sure will."

"Belle . . ." Nancy said warningly.

"Thank you, Mrs. Peeples," Clint said. "I, uh, hope I haven't gotten you into too much trouble with your friend Lisa."

Nancy smiled and said, "I can handle Lisa."

Walking out she added to herself, "At least, I used to be able to."

"Mr. Adams?" Belle said, smiling. "Will you follow me, please?"

"Lead the way, Miss Walker."

"Just call me Belle."

"I'm in your hands, Belle."

"You wish, sweetie," Belle said. "Follow me."

TWENTY-ONE

Clint took a hot bath drawn for him by Belle, who was smiling broadly when she brought him his towels.

"You want your back scrubbed, sweetie," she told him, "you just let me know, hear?"

"You'll be the first one I call, Belle," he promised.

He remembered that Vicky had told him that all of the women in Freedom had been abused in one way or other by men. Belle certainly didn't act like she had anything against men.

After the bath he dressed in fresh clothes. His gear had been brought from his rig and left in his room—including his rifle. He guessed that Nancy Peeples was going out of her way to let him know that he was trusted—or at least tolerated. He was sure that if Lisa Ford had her way he'd be getting a different message entirely.

His stomach had started growling halfway through the bath, and now that he was clean and dressed, he was starving. He looked out the window and saw the main street, as empty as if it was a ghost town.

He sat on the bed, figuring that he was better off waiting for Nancy Peeples to come back and get him like she said rather than wandering around on his own.

* * *

When Nancy went back to the jail Lisa Ford was there alone, seated behind her desk. She had a cup in her hand, but Nancy didn't smell coffee. It was more than likely Lisa was drinking whiskey from the bottle she kept in the desk.

"Lisa . . ."

Lisa looked up and frowned at Nancy.

"We have a problem, Nancy," she said.

"I know we do," Nancy said, "and we have to resolve it."

"I'm talking about this thing with Clint Adams," Lisa said. "You know who he is, don't you?"

Nancy frowned. "What do you mean?"

"You *don't* know who he is?"

"He's a man who saved Vicky's life, I know that much," Nancy said. "What are you referring to?"

"The Gunsmith, Nancy," Lisa said, "the goddamned *Gun*smith, that's what *I'm* referring to."

Nancy stopped short and stared at Lisa. "The Gunsmith?"

"*Now* you know who he is?"

"Are you sure?" Nancy asked.

"Of course I'm sure," Lisa said.

Nancy thought a moment, then shook her head. "All right," she said, "so he's the Gunsmith. I don't see where that changes anything. He's still the man who saved Vicky's life."

"So *what*?" Lisa said. "He's the man who's going to destroy Freedom for us, that's who he is."

Nancy shook her head and said, "I don't see it, Lisa. Why should he?"

"Look," Lisa said, "years ago, before he became who

he is now, he was a lawman—and once a lawman, always a lawman, I say."

"His reputation certainly doesn't bear that out," Nancy said. "Maybe he *was* a lawman once, but that was a long time ago."

"Nancy," Lisa said, "we built this up, you and I, and he's gonna bring us down."

"What did we build that's so great, Lisa?" Nancy asked. "What?"

"A world without men, that's what."

"That's your definition, Lisa," Nancy said. "I never quite had that in mind."

"Sure you did," Lisa said. "We both did. Only you've changed your mind of late."

"I haven't changed, Lisa," Nancy said. "I'm not the one who's changed. You have."

"I'm the same, Nancy," Lisa said. "Like always, I'm the one who knows what to do."

"What do you propose we do then, Lisa?" Nancy asked. "What?"

"What else?" Lisa said. "Kill him."

"Lisa!"

"Why not?" Lisa said, slamming her cup down so violently that she spilled whiskey on the desk. "It's all right for us to rob banks and get in shoot-outs while we're doin' it, but it ain't all right for us to kill to protect ourselves? Nancy, for God sake, wake up."

"Lisa," Nancy said, "we have to talk about this, and I don't have the time now."

"Sure," Lisa said. She leaned over, opened a drawer in her desk, and brought out the whiskey bottle. "Sure, Nancy," she said, pouring her cup full, "you go and play hostess to Mr. Adams. Go ahead. Talk to him, and when you decide that I'm right, you come back here and we'll talk about it. All right?"

"I'm sorry, Lisa," Nancy said. "As good as you are with a gun, you are no match for a man with a reputation like Clint Adams."

"I don't have to go up against him alone," Lisa said. "I'll get help."

"From who?"

"There are women here who can shoot well, Nancy," Lisa said. "Kate, some of the others. Believe me, we can take care of him."

"Lisa," Nancy said, heading for the door, "take it easy on that whiskey."

"Sure, Nancy," Lisa said, "sure, I'll take it real easy."

Nancy stared at Lisa Ford, then shook her head and left the office.

"Jesus!" Lisa shouted, and took a drink right from the bottle.

Nancy left the office and stopped right outside. She ran her hands through her hair and thought about Clint Adams. Of all the men Vicky could have brought back with her she had to pick the fastest, deadliest gun this country had ever known.

Before going to see Clint Adams, Nancy decided she had to talk to Vicky, no matter what Margaret Colin had said.

TWENTY-TWO

Nancy walked to the building where Vicky Tanner lived. There were so many buildings in town, and so few women living there, that each women virtually had her own place, if she so desired. Some of the women had chosen to live together, but Vicky wasn't one of them. She lived alone in a building that was once a hardware store. The storefront downstairs was still dark and empty, but Vicky lived upstairs, in two rooms that she had fixed up. The stairway to the rooms was on the side of the building, in an alley. Nancy mounted the stairs and knocked on the door.

The door was opened by Donna Murray.

"Hello, Donna," Nancy said.

Donna smiled and said, "Why was I expecting you?"

"I won't be long, Donna," Nancy promised. "I just have to ask Vicky a couple of things."

"Sure," Donna said, "she's feeling better anyway. Come on in."

"Thanks."

After forty-five minutes Clint's hunger was starting to get the best of him. He decided to go down to the hotel lobby and wait there for Nancy.

When he got downstairs Belle was behind the desk, but he noticed she had changed clothes. She was now wearing a blouse, and when she saw him she leaned her elbows on the desk. The move made her chubby breasts swell and almost pour out of the blouse. He guessed that was the effect she had been hoping for.

"Hello, Belle," Clint said.

"Mr. Adams."

"You can call me Clint, Belle," he said. "After all, you did draw me a bath, didn't you?"

"I sure did," she said. "Did you like it?"

"Best bath I ever had."

"You look better all cleaned up," she said.

"Why, thank you, Belle." He walked to the desk and leaned on it. She had also put on some kind of perfume, and he was willing to bet that most of the scent was wafting up from between her big, pillowy breasts. "Didn't Mrs. Peeples say she'd be back in half an hour?"

"I'm sure she did," Belle said. "Why? You hungry?"

"Starving."

"I'm sure she'll be here soon," Belle said. "You don't mind waiting here with me, do you?"

"Belle," he said, "why do I have the feeling you have your eye on me?"

"Maybe it's because I do, Clint."

"Ah, Belle," he said, looking pointedly at her breasts, "I'm afraid that a woman like you would just kill me."

"Maybe," she said, "but it would be a helluva way to die, wouldn't it?"

He was about to answer when Nancy came walking in. She took one look at Belle and Clint, both leaning on the desk, Belle's breasts almost out of her blouse, and shook her head.

"Belle," she said, "you have no shame."

"Why should I be ashamed?" Belle asked, standing up. "I got nothing to be ashamed of."

"No you don't, Belle," Clint said, smiling.

"Mr. Adams, you must be *very* hungry, by now."

"Yes, I am, Mrs. Peeples."

"Why don't we walk over to the cafe?"

"Just lead the way, ma'am," Clint said, straightening up. "Belle, see you later."

"Bye, sweetie."

Outside Clint fell into step beside Nancy Peeples this time rather than walking behind her.

"Is Belle giving you a hard time, Mr. Adams?" Nancy asked.

"No, ma'am," Clint said. "Nothing I can't handle."

"Hmmm . . ." Nancy said.

"What I mean is, Belle's attitude is not one I expected to find in Freedom."

"I assume Vicky explained the idea behind Freedom?"

"The general idea, yes, ma'am."

Nancy stopped short and said, "Could you stop calling me ma'am."

"Uh, yes, Mrs. Peeples."

"No, don't call me that either," Nancy said. "Oh, hell, just call me Nancy, all right?"

"All right, Nancy," Clint said. "Like I said earlier, I'm perfectly willing to cooperate."

"That's something we have to talk about, Mr. Adams," Nancy said.

"Call me Clint."

"Clint," she said.

"That's right."

Despite herself, she found herself liking Clint Adams.

"This way," she said, and started walking again.

• • •

Vicky had been shocked to learn that Clint Adams was a man with a reputation as a gunman.

"Nancy," she had said from her bed, "are you sure about this?"

"Lisa's sure," Nancy said, "and she knows about things like that—and as soon as she mentioned it, I remembered his reputation. I just didn't connect him with the Gunsmith when you said his name."

"B-but he was a perfect gentleman!" Vicky said.

"Perfect?" Donna asked.

When Vicky blushed Nancy was sure it was because she had slept with Clint Adams. She decided not to mention it just yet.

"Did anything else happen along the way, Vicky?" Nancy asked. "What else can you tell me about the man?"

"Well . . . we ran into a posse from Langton."

"You did?" Nancy said, wide-eyed. "Well, what happened?"

"Clint told me to let him do all the talking. He had the sheriff believing that we were, well, married." Vicky blushed again.

"But he didn't know that it was you who had held up the bank, did he?"

"Nancy," Vicky said, "I believe he did know."

"And he still helped you with the posse?"

"Yes."

"Hmmm," Nancy said.

"Lisa wants to kill him, doesn't she?" Donna asked.

"Nancy, no!" Vicky said. "I told him I wouldn't let anyone hurt him."

"He has to cooperate with us, Vicky," Nancy said. "if he *swears* not to give us away . . ."

"Do you think he will, Nancy?" Donna asked.

"I don't know."

"He will," Vicky said. "I know he will."

"Just like that, Vick?" Donna asked. "Even though he knows we've been breaking the law?"

"Well, maybe if we tell him we won't do it anymore?" Vicky suggested.

"And what do we do for money after that?" Nancy said.

"I think you know the answer to that, Nancy," Donna said.

Nancy frowned and said, "I'll talk to you later. Let me see what Mr. Adams has to say for himself."

"Nancy," Vicky said, "I don't want him to be hurt."

"I know, Vicky," Nancy said. "I know."

TWENTY-THREE

When they reached the cafe there were only a few women in the place eating. Nancy walked directly to a table, where she seated herself and Clint.

"We serve ourselves here," she said. "Most of our citizens just feed themselves at home, but when we don't feel like cooking we can come here. Rosie Daniels does all the cooking, but if you want something you've got to go and get it yourself."

"I see."

"She's usually in the kitchen cooking."

Clint sniffed the air, taking in the delicious cooking smells.

"What would you like?"

"A steak would be fine," he said, "or some stew."

"She usually has a pot of stew on," Nancy said. "I'll go and check."

Nancy stood up and walked to a curtained doorway, which Clint assumed led to the kitchen. As she disappeared through it he looked around at the small cafe. The other women were trying to eat their food and watch him at the same time, without *seeming* to watch him. He smiled and looked away, pretending he didn't see *them* pretending they weren't watching him.

Nancy reappeared carrying two steaming bowls of stew. She set one down in front of him, and one on her side of the table.

"I'll be right back."

She went back to the kitchen and reappeared with a basket of biscuits.

"One more trip," she said.

"I can help . . ." he started, but she stopped him.

"No, you sit right there," she said. "I'll be right back."

She returned with two mugs of beer. "I hope beer is all right."

"Beer's fine."

"Afterward, if you like," she said, seating herself, "we can have some coffee."

"That's great."

He tasted the stew, found it delicious, and said so.

"Rosie will be glad to hear it."

They continued to eat.

"Clint . . . we have a problem."

"*You* do?" he asked. "Or *we* do?" He pointed to her.

"Well," she said, regarding him across the table, "we all do, I guess."

"What to do about me?"

"Yes," she said. "Vicky never should have brought you here."

"She mentioned that," he said. "She offered to walk part of the way, once we got near, but I insisted on bringing her in. I don't think a long walk would have done her much good, do you, Nancy?"

"No, you're right about that," Nancy said. "According to Margaret, you made all the right decisions regarding Vicky's wound."

"And now you have to make the right decisions regarding me . . . right?"

"Not just me."

Clint almost said, "You mean the Seven?" but decided not to let Nancy know that Vicky had told him about them. That might get Vicky into more trouble than she was already in.

"There are others who will be in on the decision," Nancy said.

"What decision is that, Nancy?"

"About . . . what to do with you." She was looking down at her plate as she spoke.

"What about what *I* want?" he asked.

Nancy stopped eating and took a deep breath, then looked up at him.

"Clint, we know who you are," she said. "I know what you're capable of. You could probably kill a lot of us with little or no problem—"

"Hey, whoa," he said, dropping his fork and holding his hand out. "What are we talking about here? I'm not looking to kill anyone, Nancy. And you'll pardon me for saying so, but you *don't* know what I'm capable of, and you certainly don't know who I am. All you know is what you've heard, or read, or been told. Am I right?"

"Well . . . yes."

"You didn't even know that I had a reputation when we were first introduced, did you?"

"Well . . . no."

"Who told you?"

"Lisa did," Nancy said. "She knows about things like that."

"I see," Clint said. "And what does Lisa want to do about me?"

"She . . ."

"She wants to kill me, right?"

"Yes," Nancy said, her voice barely audible.

"Nancy," Clint said, "can I tell you what I think is best for all of us?"

"Yes," she said, "of course."

"I think I should just leave in the morning," he said, "and never look back."

"Would you . . . tell anyone about us?"

"No, why should I?" Clint said. "I don't have any proof that anyone from this town has done anything wrong."

"That's . . . true," Nancy said. She hadn't realized that. No one had actually *told* him that they robbed banks to get their money—at least, Vicky *claimed* that she hadn't told him that.

"So what are you all worried about?" he asked. "I'm not a threat to you, Nancy, believe me. I wish you'd believe that, and I wish you'd convince others—Lisa, and any others who think so—that I'm not."

"Can I ask you a question?" she asked.

"Sure, go ahead."

"If someone, a lawman, asked you if you had any information about . . . robberies, bank robberies, what would you say?"

"I'd say no."

"And if a lawman asked you if you had any . . . suspicions regarding certain . . . robberies, what would you say?"

What he *should* have said immediately was, "Nothing," but what he actually said was nothing—he hesitated for a moment, and that was long enough for Nancy Peeples to decide that maybe they did have a problem after all.

"Damn," she said under her breath.

TWENTY-FOUR

They finished their dinner in relative silence, and then walked back to the hotel the same way.

"We can talk again tomorrow," Nancy said outside the hotel.

"Do I have to watch my back tonight, Nancy?" Clint asked.

She hesitated before saying, "No, I don't think so."

"What about Lisa?"

"I don't think she'll do anything on her own, Clint," Nancy said. "We have a sort of group here that makes the decisions. We'll meet tomorrow."

"I see."

"I hope you're not . . . planning on doing anything tonight."

"I'm planning on staying alive, Nancy," Clint said, "but that's a plan I always have. Do you understand?"

"Yes," she said, "yes, I do."

"I'll be here tomorrow," he said, "but I can't promise much after that."

"All right," she said, "that's fair enough. We'll talk tomorrow."

"Good night then," he said. "Thanks for dinner."

"You're welcome," she said, "and good night."

He went into the hotel and found Belle behind the desk. She was still wearing the blouse.

"Good dinner?" she asked.

"Fine," he said.

"Goin' to your room?"

"That's what I planned to do, yes."

"Alone?"

"Why Belle," he said, "is that an offer?"

"Darned tootin'," she said.

"Like I said before, Belle," he said, "I just wouldn't trust my heart with a gal like you. It just might burst from pleasure."

She put her chin in her hands and said, "You change your mind during the night, you let me know, all right? My room's in the back."

"I'll let you know, Belle. Good night."

"Good night, Clint."

He went up the stairs, his back itching because he knew she was watching him. When he reached the second floor he wondered if his was the only room in the hotel that was occupied. He listened intently, but didn't hear anything. He walked to his room and opened the door, then stopped short when he realized that someone was inside, on the bed, waiting for him.

"It's only me," a tiny voice said.

"It might be better if you lit the lamp next to the bed," Clint said from the doorway.

"All right," she said, "but I wanted it to be a surprise."

He heard the match strike and watched as she lit the lamp, then turned it up. He remembered seeing the girl in the bed when he first came to town. She was young, with long brown hair and a pixieish face with a turned-up nose. She was holding the sheet up to her chin, which was just as well.

"What's your name?" he asked.

"Nia."

"How old are you?"

"Nineteen."

"Nineteen?"

"Well . . . almost eighteen."

"That means you're seventeen, right?"

"Only for three more months."

He stepped inside, but left the door open.

"Your mother's the doctor, right?"

"A nurse," Nia said, "but she does the doctorin' around here."

"Nia," he said, "I don't think you should be here."

"I ain't never been with a man," she said.

"I don't doubt it."

"And I'm of an age when I'm thinkin' about men, only there ain't none hereabouts."

"So I understand."

Now she dropped the sheet and he saw her breasts. They were small and round, with brown nipples. She might have been young, but there wasn't an ounce of baby fat on her.

"Nia . . ."

"Ain't I pretty enough for you?" she asked.

"Nia, you're very pretty."

"Then you'll make love to me?"

He saw her clothes on the floor next to the bed and walked over to them. She thought he was coming to bed, and moved over to make room. Instead, he bent over, picked up her clothes, and tossed them onto the bed.

"I'm sorry, Nia, but no, I won't."

"Why not?" Nia asked. "Is it Vicky?"

"It's not Vicky or anyone else, Nia," he said. "You're just too young."

Nia pouted and then said, "I could tell my mother you *made* me come up here. I could tell Lisa you *forced* me to come up here, and then you . . . you . . ."

"That wouldn't be nice, would it, Nia?"

She stared at him, then lowered her head.

"No, it wouldn't . . . I guess."

"You better get dressed," he said, and turned to look out the window. He heard her get out of bed and start to dress.

"I don't wanna be here, you know," she said. "In Freedom, I mean."

"Maybe you should talk to your mother about that, Nia," he said.

"I don't like it here."

"Well," he said, "in three months you'll be eighteen, and you can leave if you want."

"You bet I will," she said. "All right, I'm dressed. You can turn around."

He did, and was pleased to find that she was totally clad.

"You wouldn't take me with you when you leave, would you?" she asked.

"I couldn't do that."

"No, I guess not," Nia said. "Besides, you probably *won't* leave here."

"Why not?"

"I don't think Lisa is gonna let you," she said, coming closer to him. "I think she's gonna kill you. It's a shame, really, 'cause you're real good-looking."

She reached up quickly, clasped her hands behind his neck, pulled his head down, and kissed him awkwardly.

He put his arms around her, drew her close, and kissed her properly, showing her how.

"God . . ." she said breathlessly, "I ain't never been kissed before."

"Well, now you know how," he said, releasing her.

She walked to the door with her hands shoved into her back pockets and her back arched. When she got there she turned and looked at him again sadly.

"It's a shame Lisa's gonna kill you," she said.

"I think so too," he said.

"Night."

She walked out and closed the door gently behind her. Clint took a deep breath. It had been a long time since he had kissed a girl that young. He had liked it way too much. He could still taste her mouth, feel her vibrant young body pressed against his.

"Dirty old buzzard," he scolded himself.

TWENTY-FIVE

Well, so far he had found two women in Freedom who didn't hate men, Belle and Nia. He also didn't think that Vicky hated him, so that was three out of twenty-five. Maybe Freedom wasn't the Utopia most of the women wanted. It certainly wasn't what those three women wanted, and Clint had a feeling it wasn't what Nancy Peeples wanted either. Lisa Ford, however—there was a different story.

He was lying on the bed, and now he decided that before he went to sleep he'd better make sure that no one would surprise him during the night.

He took the straight-backed chair and jammed the back of it underneath the doorknob. Now even if someone kicked the door it wouldn't open, not right away. Next he took the pitcher and bowl and balanced them on the windowsill. Anyone trying to get in would knock them over, setting up a racket that would wake the dead.

That done he took off his boots, hung his gunbelt on the bedpost, and lay down to go to sleep.

Lisa Ford sat in her office with an empty bottle of

whiskey. She looked through the desk drawers for the tenth time, and still did not find another bottle.

Shit, she thought, if this was a real town she could walk over to the saloon and get a drink. Well, when she finally took over that was the first thing she was going to do, open up a real saloon.

The door to her office opened and she looked up to see who it was.

"Oh, it's you," she said, squinting to see through the alcoholic haze. "Whataya want?"

"Nothing," the person said. "I just came to see how you were."

"I'm just fine," Lisa said. "If I had another bottle of whiskey, I'd be even better."

She watched as the person approached the desk, and then moved around behind it.

"Did you check the drawers?" the person asked.

"Hey," Lisa said, forgetting that she had already done that ten times, "that's a good idea."

She leancd over to look through the desk drawers, but when something hit her in the back of the head she dove into one of the drawers instead, and then fell into total blackness . . .

TWENTY-SIX

When Clint awoke the next morning his intentions were as follows: have breakfast, say good-bye to Vicky and make sure she was all right, talk to Nancy Peeples briefly, and then leave the town of Freedom behind him. He hoped that no one would ever ask him if he knew—or thought he knew—anything pertaining to the bank robberies that took place in the towns of Benbow and Langton, Kansas. He hoped never to be faced with the moral dilemma of having to answer such questions.

After he dressed he went downstairs, and was surprised not to see Belle behind the front desk. In fact, no one was behind the front desk.

He walked down the street to the small cafe without encountering anyone, and was surprised to find that the cafe was closed. Maybe it just didn't open that early. And maybe there was no one on the street because they were all asleep. Sure, and maybe this feeling he had that something was wrong was just that, a feeling and nothing more.

He decided to go right to his last intention, which was to leave Freedom. Since he and Vicky had not passed a livery stable when they entered town, he surmised that it must be at the other end of town. He walked that way, and before long came to the stable. The front doors were closed, and as he approached he could see that they were padlocked.

Something was definitely wrong.

He examined the lock and found that it was a thick one. He'd need a sledgehammer to break it. He wasn't sure that shooting it would help, and he decided to save that option for later.

He turned around and walked back the way he had come. Since he'd come to Freedom he had only been to three places in town: the hotel, the cafe, and the jail. He had already seen the hotel and cafe this morning, so he decided to try the jail. Maybe he'd find somebody there that he could talk to.

He walked to the jail, tried the door, and found it locked.

"Shit," he said.

His rig and his team—not to mention Duke—were locked away where he couldn't get to them, and there was no one around for him to talk to. He could do one of two things. He could start knocking on doors, or he could simply walk out into the center of the street and call out.

He decided not to knock on doors. There was no guarantee that anyone would answer, and he certainly didn't intend to start kicking doors in—not yet anyway.

He walked out in the center of the street and stood there with his hands on his hips. It was very possible that there were twenty-five sets of eyes on him right at that moment—either that, or everyone in town had left and he was alone.

"Hello!" he called out.

No answer.

"Anybody here?" he called. "Vicky? Nancy? Anyone?"

Still no answer, but he thought he caught a glimpse of a curtain in a window, as if someone had been looking out and then ducked back abruptly.

"Come on!" he shouted. "Someone has to come out and talk to me! Nancy?"

He waited, listening intently, and suddenly he heard the sound of a door opening. He turned in that direction and saw Nancy coming out the door of what was once a general store.

"Nancy," he said. "What's going on?"

She stood just in front of the door, her shoulders hunched as if she expected to be struck a blow.

"You don't know?" she asked.

"I don't know what?" he asked. "Nancy, what's wrong?"

"Clint . . . there are more than a dozen rifles trained on you right now."

He looked around, but could see nothing, and no one. If they were aiming rifles at him, it was from behind closed doors and windows.

"Why is that, Nancy?"

She hesitated, and then said, "Are you claiming that you don't know?"

"Don't know what?" he asked. "I can't claim not to know anything unless you tell me what I'm claiming not to know—and now I've got myself confused! Nancy, just tell me what's going on."

"Somebody was killed last night," she said.

"Killed?" he asked. "Who was killed?"

She didn't answer right away.

"Nancy, is Vicky all right?"

"Vicky is fine," Nancy answered.

"Then who was killed?"

"It was Lisa," she said. "Lisa Ford was killed."

The one woman in town who wanted to kill him!

"And you think I did it?"

"Yes . . . that's what a lot of us think."

"Well, I didn't, Nancy," he said. "I didn't leave the hotel all night."

She didn't reply.

"How can I prove that to you?"

"I—I don't know . . ."

"Well, I don't know either," he said. "Look, you've got my rig locked up, or I'd leave town—or maybe you'd just rather shoot me down here in the street. Is that what you want?"

"It's not what *I* want," she said.

"Well, let's make a move here then, Nancy," Clint said. "Either tell your people to shoot, or let me help find out who *did* kill Lisa."

She didn't move, or answer.

"What's it going to be, Nancy?" he asked, spreading his arms out. He didn't seriously think there was anyone in town who was going to shoot him.

He hoped.

TWENTY-SEVEN

Nancy walked Clint over to the jail and unlocked the door. As they entered, he saw Lisa Ford's body lying behind the desk.

"Is that how you found her?"

"That's how Kate found her, yes," Nancy said.

"Close the door," he said, and approached the desk and the body.

He leaned over and examined the dead woman, moving only her head.

"How did she die?" Nancy asked.

"Well," he said, probing the body's head, "she has a bump on the back of her head, but that's not what killed her. Someone knocked her out from behind, and then it looks like they strangled her with a piece of rope. See here?"

"I'd rather not look," Nancy said, averting her eyes.

"All right," he said, "but if you did look you'd see the mark of the rope around her neck."

He stood up and stared down at Nancy.

"Am I the only one in town with a supposed motive to kill her?" he asked.

"Of course—"

"Think before you answer, Nancy," Clint said. "I get the feeling that Lisa was a forceful person, used to getting her own way. People like that tend to make enemies."

Nancy opened her mouth to answer, then stopped.

"Can we go outside?" she asked.

"In a minute," he said.

He went into the back where the cells were and looked around. He tried the back door and found it bolted from the inside.

"The back door is locked from the inside," he said. "If the killer came in that way, Lisa let them in and then bolted the door. Was the front door locked or unlocked when Kate came by this morning?"

"You'll have to ask her."

"More than likely it was unlocked," Clint said. "At least I *hope* it was."

"Why?"

"If it was locked, then that would mean that someone killed Lisa, got out, and left both doors locked from the inside."

"B-but . . . that's impossible."

"Right," he said. "So that means the door was probably unlocked, and if the killer came and went through the front door, then Lisa knew her killer."

"You mean . . . one of us killed her?"

"Unless there's a stranger in town that none of you has seen," he said.

"This is making me dizzy," she said. "Can we step outside now?"

"Sure."

They went back outside and locked the door.

"All right, yes, you're right," Nancy said. "Lisa *was* like that."

"Then who did she *not* get along with?"

"A few people," Nancy said, "me included."

"You and she had the idea for Freedom, didn't you?" he asked.

"Yes."

"Then I would have thought you and she would be good friends."

"We were," Nancy said, "at one time, but things had changed recently."

"Changed how?"

Nancy rubbed her palms on her thighs and looked up and down the street.

"Listen," Clint said, "why don't you tell everyone to come out of hiding, maybe get some people to move her body someplace. After that we can sit down together somewhere and talk."

"That's a good idea," Nancy said.

"Also, see if you can bring Kate along. I'd like to talk to her."

"Right."

"Nancy," Clint said, "I didn't kill Lisa. If I had, I don't think I would have done it that way . . . do you? I mean, it wouldn't be in keeping with my reputation, would it?"

"I suppose not," she said. "Look, I'm sorry about what I said yesterday . . . about the kind of person you are. You were right, I *don't* know who you are, or what kind of man you are, but I do believe that you wouldn't have had to sneak up behind Lisa to kill her."

"Okay," he said, "so now we both don't think I did it . . ."

"Right."

"Did *you?*"

"What?" She looked at him in shock.

"Somebody killed her, Nancy," he said, spreading his hands, "someone she knew. Think about that. It could have been anyone."

"But . . . me?"

He raised his hands and said, "I was just asking. Why don't we meet at that little cafe in half an hour?"

"A-all right."

"Uh, it will be open, won't it?"

"Yes," she said, "it will be open."

"And try to think who would have had a motive to kill Lisa," he said. "I don't mean someone she may have quarreled with. I mean someone with a *real* motive, someone who was in her way."

"I-I'll try . . ."

"I'll be in my hotel room," he said. He thought it better if he went indoors for a while and gave the women time to adjust to not having to hide from him anymore.

TWENTY-EIGHT

A half an hour later Clint was sitting in the cafe with Nancy and Kate. There was no one else in the place, except possibly for Rosie, the cook. At least, *someone* had made breakfast, which Nancy and Kate had brought to the table for him. Neither of them was eating. They were both lingering over cups of coffee.

"Tell me what happened this morning, Kate," Clint said. He couldn't help eating. He had seen death many times before, and today it hadn't diminished his appetite.

"I went over to the office, like I do every day," Kate said.

"What time?"

"It was about seven a.m."

"Okay, go on."

"There ain't much to tell," she said. "I walked in and found Lisa lying behind the desk."

"You walked right in? The door wasn't locked?"

"No, it was unlocked."

"And what about the back door?"

"I—I didn't look at the back door."

"You didn't bolt it?"

"No."

"What did you do after you found Lisa?"

"I went and got Nancy."

Clint looked at Nancy, who took up the story then. "I went back to the office with Kate and looked at Lisa."

"Did you touch her?"

"No."

"What then?"

"We both got out of there and locked the door, and then I called a meeting of the Seven."

"The Seven?" He still didn't want her to know that Vicky had told him about the Seven.

"Well . . . there are only six of us now," Nancy said, "but the Seven is what we called ourselves, the seven of us who actually founded Freedom."

"I thought you and Lisa founded it."

"The idea was originally ours, but there were seven of us who made it work."

"All right, slow down here a minute," he said. "Who were the original seven? You and Lisa . . ."

"Right . . . Kate, Donna Murray, Barbara Petty, Jan Grape, and Ori Hardy."

"Have I met them?"

"Donna was with me when you rode in. She walked Vicky over to Margaret Colin's."

Clint remembered her, a pretty dark-haired woman.

"All right . . . and the others?"

"I don't think you've met any of them."

"Okay," he said, "so you called a meeting. Then what?"

"Well . . . we decided that you were the one who must have killed Lisa."

"Why?"

"Because you knew that she wanted to kill you."

"I only heard that from you, Nancy," Clint said.

"I know," she said defensively. "I admit I may have been the one who mentioned you as the killer . . . but I wasn't thinking straight."

"What makes you think he isn't the killer?" Kate asked. "He can't *prove* that he didn't do it."

For a moment Clint wished he *had* let Nia stay with him last night. It would have given him a perfect witness to the fact that he had never left his room. Thinking of Nia also reminded him that the young girl had also told him that Lisa was going to kill him. He decided not to mention that at all.

"Kate, he wouldn't have had to sneak up on her to kill her."

"He would if he wanted it to look like one of us did it," Kate said. "Come on, Nancy, who of us would want to kill Lisa?"

"Looking at it from the outside?" Clint said. "I'd say Nancy had a motive."

"What?" Nancy said.

"You said you and she weren't getting along lately. Could that be because her idea of what Freedom should be and your idea just weren't the same anymore?"

Nancy stared at Clint, but Kate looked at Nancy. She knew that she and Lisa had been talking about ousting Nancy as mayor, and now she felt guilty about it. Still, if Nancy had somehow found out about that, *would* she have killed Lisa?

"Why are you looking at me like that?" Nancy asked Kate.

"No reason," Kate said, averting her eyes. "Sorry."

"What about Vicky?" Clint asked.

"Vicky is in bed," Kate said.

"I'm just suggesting possibilities," Clint said. "Vicky promised me I wouldn't be hurt. What would she have done if she knew that Lisa wanted to kill me?"

"She wouldn't have *killed* her," Kate said.

"Maybe, maybe not," Clint said.

"Nancy, don't you see what he's doing?" Kate asked. "He's trying to get us to suspect each other."

"Kate's right, Nancy," Clint said, "I *do* want you to suspect each other, because I know I didn't kill Lisa, which means one of you did."

"I've heard enough," Kate said. She stood up and stormed out of the cafe.

"You're saying there are twenty-four possible killers in town," Nancy said.

"Twenty-four possibilities," he said, "but how many probabilities? If you were looking at this objectively, would you say you had a possible motive to kill Lisa? What if she was planning to replace you?"

Nancy fidgeted uncomfortably and said, "I think she was."

"With who?"

"The only possibility would be Kate," Nancy said. "She and Lisa were close."

"Well," he said, "if Lisa was planning on replacing you with Kate, that would leave Kate out as a suspect. So now we've reduced it to twenty-three. Let's see if we can't get it down further."

TWENTY-NINE

They spent the next hour trying to come up with a realistic list of people who might have had a motive to kill Lisa Ford.

In the beginning it was difficult for Nancy, so Clint had to talk her through it.

"Who had she argued with recently?" he asked.

"Well . . . we were taking about Vicky being missing, and Lisa did not want to send anyone out to look for her."

"And who did?"

"Well, Donna Murray. I mean, she was Vicky's sponsor, and she had volunteered to go out and find her if she wasn't back by Saturday."

"What else?"

"Well . . . I walked into Margaret's office and Lisa and Donna were shouting at each other. Donna said she wasn't going to let Lisa bully her anymore."

"You see?" Clint said. "If you try hard enough you can come up with motives. We've eliminated Kate, and we've put Donna at the top of the list."

"And me."

"Right," Clint said, "and you. Now who else?"

"I don't know."

"Let's put it this way," Clint said. "If Lisa was to try to replace you as mayor, would it take a vote?"

"Yes."

"Who would vote with you?"

"Well, Donna, Barbara, and Jan would probably vote with me," Nancy said.

"That leaves . . . Kate and Ori to vote with Lisa, right?"

"That's right."

"So Lisa would have to win over either Donna, Barbara, or Jan, right?"

"Right."

"And she could forget about Donna, so that leaves Barbara or Jan. If she had approached them about voting with her, they'd know that she was planning to try and oust you. That might give them a motive."

"They'd kill her to keep her from replacing me?"

He shrugged and said, "We're just dealing with possibilities here."

"Well, if we're going to deal with possibilities, you might as well put Margaret on the list."

"Margaret? Why?"

"Lisa wanted to bring a real doctor into town. That would reduce Margaret to being just a nurse again."

"I thought she was a nurse."

"She is, but she's kind of gotten used to being our doctor."

"All right, so Margaret goes on the list, and that would mean we'd have to put Nia on the list too."

"Nia?" Nancy said. "She's a child!"

"She's not such a child, Nancy," Clint said. "When I got back to my room last night she was in my bed naked."

"Nia?"

"That's right."

"Clint, you didn't—"

"No, I didn't," he said. "I made her get dressed and get out. I would have taken Belle into my bed before Nia— and before you ask, *no*, I didn't do that either."

"I wasn't going to ask," Nancy said, looking amused for the first time that morning.

"Of course, if I *had* let Nia stay, she'd be able to prove I didn't kill Lisa. As it stands now, she becomes a suspect as well. Let's see what we have. You, Vicky, Barbara, Jan, Margaret, Nia . . . anyone else?"

"Vicky should be disregarded," Nancy said. "She's hurt."

"Maybe Vicky and Donna did it together," he said. "How close are they anyway?"

"Pretty close," Nancy said. "As a matter of fact, they're cousins."

"Is that generally known?"

"Well . . . no," Nancy said. "It's sort of an unwritten rule that we don't sponsor relatives."

"What about Margaret and Nia?"

"They came to town together."

"And what if Lisa found out that Donna and Vicky were cousins?"

"She'd have made a big stink."

"And if she could prove that you knew, that would help her get you out, wouldn't it?"

"Yes . . . giving me another strong motive to kill her, right?"

"Or Donna and Vicky," he said. "What about the other women in town? Did they get along with Lisa?"

"Some better than others," Nancy said. "Belle didn't like Lisa."

"Why not?"

"Lisa made fun of her," Nancy said. "You probably saw for yourself that Lisa was the most beautiful woman in Freedom."

"I saw."

"She teased Belle a lot about being . . . fat."

"Belle's not fat," Clint said, "she's just a little . . . big."

"Well, Lisa used to tease her."

"What is Belle doing here anyway?" Clint asked. "She doesn't strike me as a man-hater."

"She's not. . . a *lot* of us aren't," Nancy said. "Some of us just see this as a haven, a place to hide for a while. In fact, some of us wanted to call the town Haven, but . . ."

"But what?"

She averted her eyes and said, "Lisa was adamant about calling it Freedom, and I gave in."

Another point of dissension between them.

"I think we'd better call it a morning, Nancy," Clint said.

"All right," she said, "but what do we do now?"

"That's up to you," he said. "You're in charge now. What do you want to do?"

"I want to find out who killed Lisa," Nancy said. "And you probably want to be on your way."

"I'm not going to leave until we *do* find out who killed Lisa," Clint said. "I don't want to leave here with a cloud over my head. The only way for me to really prove I *didn't* do it is to find out who *did*."

"I'm glad you're going to stay," she said. "I don't think I could do it by myself."

"For what it's worth, Nancy," he said, "I don't think you killed her."

"Thank you, Clint," she said. "That means a lot to me."

"But I think it's time we found who *did*."

THIRTY

Clint told Nancy that he wanted to talk to Vicky. She offered to take him to her rooms, but he thought it would be better if she just told him where Vicky lived.

"What should I do while you're talking to her?" Nancy asked.

"See about Lisa's body," he said. "I'm sure you'll want to bury her. Do you have someplace to do that?"

"I . . . we never thought about . . . dying . . ."

"Well, if you're going to keep Freedom going that's something you're going to have to think about," he said. "People are going to die, and they're going to have to be buried someplace."

"I'll meet with the others," she said.

"Don't have a meeting yet," he said. "I want to be there. Just see that the body is taken care of."

"All right. Shall I talk to anyone?"

"No," he said. "I want to talk to Vicky alone, but we can talk to everyone together."

"All right," she said. "I'll wait for you at the town hall when I'm finished."

"Fine," he said. "I'll see you there."

121

They separated, and Clint followed her directions to the building where Vicky lived. He mounted the steps and knocked. Donna Murray answered, and for a moment he thought he saw fear in her eyes. There were probably still a lot of women in town who thought that he was the one who killed Lisa.

"Hello," Clint said, "you're Donna."

"That's right."

"I'd like to talk to your cousin alone."

Donna frowned and said, "How did you know—oh, Nancy told you?"

"That's right."

"Where is she?"

"She'll be at the town hall in a little while," Clint said. "Right now she's seeing to Lisa's body."

"I'd better go and see her," Donna said, and then she looked over her shoulder at Vicky.

"I'll be fine, Donna," Vicky said. "Go ahead."

Donna hesitated, looking again at Clint in a way that told him she still wasn't sure of him.

"Oh, go on, Donna," Vicky said. "Clint didn't kill Lisa. I *know* that."

"I'll be back in a little while," Donna said, and stepped outside. Clint closed the door and approached the bed.

Vicky sat up and held her arms out to him. He sat on the bed and held her.

"It's horrible," she said. "Who would want to kill Lisa?"

"That's what I wanted to ask you, Vicky," he said. Holding her warm body close to him was doing things to him, but he had to ignore them.

He moved back from her, but held onto her hands.

"Vicky, I know you better than I know anyone else here. I'm going to have to trust your judgment."

She took one of her hands back from him and wiped tears from her face.

"You can trust me," she said, "just like I know I can trust you."

"All right then," he said. "Who would want to kill Lisa?"

"No one."

"That's not what I want to hear," he said. "Stop thinking with your emotions. I only knew her a short time, but I've already figured out that Lisa was not an easy woman to like."

"Well . . . that's true."

"Then who disliked her enough to want to kill her?" he asked.

"I can't think of anyone . . ."

"What about Donna?"

She pulled her hand away from him and said, "Why are you asking about Donna?"

"She's your cousin," Clint said. "If Lisa found out about that she would have made a fuss."

"Yes, but—"

"Also, Donna had an argument with Lisa in the doctor—I mean, the nurse's office."

Vicky frowned and said, "I heard them shouting."

"Also," Clint said, "Lisa did not want to send anyone out to look for you when you didn't return."

Vicky made a face and said, "That would have been just like Lisa."

"You see?" he said. "*You* didn't like her."

"No, I didn't," she said, but then her eyes widened. "But that doesn't mean I killed her."

"No, it doesn't," he said, "but it means that there are a lot of people who disliked her, like you, like Donna . . .

and people who weren't getting along with her so well anymore, like Nancy."

"Nancy?" she said. "You think Nancy might have killed her?"

"Actually, I *don't* think Nancy wanted to kill her, but it appears that Lisa was going to try to replace Nancy. Who would have been against that if they knew?"

"A lot of people," she said. "Jan Grape, for one. She would have preferred to have *Lisa* replaced."

"All right," he said, "there's Jan. Who else?"

"Oh, God, Clint, I didn't mean that I thought Jan might have killed her—"

"Vicky," Clint said, holding both her hands again, but tightly, "*some*body killed her, and I have to try to figure out who. There are still a lot of people who think *I* did it. I can't leave until I find out who did."

"I understand," she said.

"Think about it for a while," Clint said. He released her hands and stood up. "How are you feeling?"

"Oh, I'm fine," she said. "Margaret said you saved my life. I told her I knew that. I'm well enough now to get up and help you."

"No, I want you to stay in bed. Just think about what we just talked about and I'll come back and see if you have any ideas."

"All right," she said, "but come back tonight. I'll try to get Donna to leave, and . . ." She blushed, and looked down at her hands.

"I'll see you later," he promised. He leaned over and kissed her forehead, and then left.

He went outside and down the stairs. Under normal circumstances he certainly would have liked to visit Vicky that evening, and sleep with her, but these weren't normal circumstances. Besides which, as much as he liked Vicky, he was finding himself more and more attracted to Nancy Peeples.

Being the only man in a town filled with women certainly did make life interesting.

THIRTY-ONE

When Clint reached the town hall Nancy was waiting outside for him.

"They're all inside," she told him.

"Kate too?"

"Yes," she said, "but she's talking to them."

"That's all right," he said. "Come on, let's go inside."

They entered, and found four women sitting at the meeting table. The fifth, Kate, was standing, and had been talking just before they entered. She stopped short when they walked in.

"Clint Adams," Nancy said, "that's Jan Grape, Barbara Petty, and Ori Hardy. You know Donna and Kate."

"Kate tells us you think one of us killed Lisa," Jan said.

"That's right," Clint said. "That is, not one of *you* specifically, but someone from town."

"Why not you?" Jan asked.

"It *could* be me," Clint said, "but I'm telling you that I didn't do it. It's up to you whether you want to believe me or not."

"Well, I don't," Kate said. She stepped away from the corner she'd been standing in, and Clint saw that she was wearing a gun on her hip. It looked too big for her. Clint guessed that it was Lisa's gun.

"If you're going to use that gun you'd better do it now," Clint said.

Kate stared at Clint and then licked her full lips.

"I'll use it when I'm ready," she said, "don't worry." The false bravado in her voice was plain for all to hear.

"Don't be ridiculous, Kate," Nancy said. "You'd be dead before you could even touch it." Nancy faced the other women and said, "I believe that Clint didn't kill Lisa. If he had, he wouldn't have sneaked up behind her to do it."

"Like I said before," Kate said, speaking to the room at large, "he could have wanted to make it look like one of us did it."

"If he did it," Nancy said, "he could have left a long time ago."

"His wagon and horses are locked up in the livery," Kate said.

"You think he couldn't get them out if he wanted to?" Nancy asked. "The fact that he's still here, trying to find out who killed Lisa, tells me that he didn't do it. It should tell you all the same thing."

They all digested that for a few moments, and then the oldest of them, Jan, spoke.

"All right," she said, "suppose we all accept that he didn't do it. Who did?"

"Somebody who didn't like Lisa," Clint said. "Someone she argued with. Someone with something to gain."

"I argued with her," Donna said, "but I wouldn't

have anything to gain by killing her."

"I think we need to find someone who fills all three criteria," Clint said.

"Of late," Jan said, looking around the table, "I don't think any of us got along with Lisa very well."

"I did," Kate said. "She was my best friend."

"I didn't have a beef with her," Barbara Petty said.

"I may not have cared for her," Ori said, "but I had nothing to gain by killing her."

"You *all* had something to gain," Kate blurted out.

"Like what?" Nancy asked.

"You all knew how Lisa felt about Freedom," Kate said. "And you knew that she and Nancy disagreed on almost everything."

"So?" Jan said.

"So . . . you knew that she wanted to replace Nancy as mayor."

"*She* wanted to replace her?" Jan asked.

"Well, not with herself. She didn't want to be mayor."

"She wanted to replace me with you?" Nancy asked.

"What's wrong with that?" Kate asked.

"Nothing," Nancy said. "Hey, after this is all over, Kate, if you want to be mayor, be my guest."

"Nancy," Jan said, "we need you to be in charge."

"Well, maybe I'm tired of being in charge," Nancy said. "Maybe I've had enough of being in charge, *and* with even being here."

With that she turned and stalked out of the room. Donna started to get up, but Jan stopped her.

"Let her go," Jan said. "She's been under a lot of pressure." She looked at Clint. "Mr. Adams, do you intend to stay here until you find out who killed Lisa?"

"Yes, I do."

"You don't have to, you know," Jan said. "You could leave."

"I *could*," Clint admitted, "but there would still be those who thought I killed her. I wouldn't like to leave with the matter unresolved."

"All right then," Jan said. "We're at your disposal. Ask us anything you want."

"Is there a room where I can talk with each of you privately?"

"Yes," Jan said, "behind this one. Would you like to start with me?"

"Sure," Clint said.

Jan stood up and said, "Follow me. The rest of you can wait here until I'm done. Decide among yourselves who will go next."

"I'm not gonna be questioned!" Kate said.

"We are going to cooperate, Kate," Jan said. "We all want to know who killed Lisa, don't we?"

Kate didn't answer. She folded her arms across her chest and glared, but she remained in the room, as did the others.

THIRTY-TWO

Clint questioned them all in private and asked them the same questions: How did they get along with Lisa? Did they want Lisa to give up her position? Would they want Nancy or Lisa to be in sole charge of Freedom? Where were they the night Lisa was killed? Had they ever killed anyone before?

They all answered the first question roughly the same way. They got along with her fairly well, as long as they didn't strongly oppose her on any issues. Kate said she got along with Lisa all the time.

Kate said she wanted Lisa to keep her job, and would have chosen Lisa over Nancy anytime. Jan said that Lisa was ideally suited to her job, more so than anyone else in town. She preferred having Lisa *and* Nancy in charge. They balanced each other out. Donna said she would have liked Nancy in sole charge. Barbara and Ori seemed to like things the way they were.

As for the question of where they were when Lisa was killed, they all said they were home in bed alone—except for Donna. She said she spent the night at Vicky's to take care of her. At this time the others were still unaware that Donna and Vicky were cousins.

So Donna was the only one with an alibi for the time Lisa was killed—although Clint still had to ask Nancy for one.

After he had finished questioning all of them he came back into the meeting room with Donna, who he had questioned last.

"All right," he said, "thanks for your cooperation. You can all go."

"What, you don't know who did it yet?" Kate asked.

"When I do, Kate," Clint said, "I'll let you know."

Kate stormed out of the room ahead of the others, who filed out in a more orderly fashion. When they were gone Clint sat down at the big table by himself. His best suspects were still Nancy and Donna. Nancy because Lisa was going to try to take Freedom over completely—with the help of Kate Dougherty—and Donna because she was the one who'd been heard arguing with Lisa, saying that she wouldn't be "bullied."

Nancy walked in at that point, appearing somewhat contrite.

"I'm sorry I stormed out," she said. "I was just . . . feeling the pressure."

"That's all right."

"You want to ask me the same questions you asked the others?" she asked, sitting down.

"Just where you were last night when Lisa was killed," Clint said.

"I was in bed," she said.

"Anyone there?"

"No," she said. "I live alone. I guess that means I don't have an alibi."

"Join the club," he said. "No one has an alibi but Donna, and she's still my number-one suspect."

"You're being nice," Nancy said. "*I'm* your number-one suspect."

"Let's say it's a tie for now," Clint said.

"What's next?"

"I'll move around town and talk to some of the other women," he said. "Maybe I'll hear something that will help. Maybe there was someone else who disliked Lisa enough to kill her."

Nancy shook her head sadly.

"I thought I knew every woman here, Clint," she said. "I can't imagine *who* killed her, but whoever it turns out to be, I'll be shocked."

"I'd better get to it," Clint said. "Would you like to meet for dinner?"

"Sure," she said. "At the cafe?"

"Fine," he said. "About six?"

"Okay," she said, standing up. "I don't know what I'll do until then."

"Do what you normally do."

She looked at him quickly, and then looked away. What she probably did right after a robbery was tend to the money. Clint wished he could talk to her about the robberies. He would like to have known whose idea they were. Hers? Lisa's? Both? Had the idea come from the Seven? Nancy certainly seemed uncomfortable with the robberies—or was it just now? After everything that had happened?

"I don't know," she said. "It'll be kind of hard to go about business as usual. I'll be looking at everyone in a different light until we find who the killer is."

"Well, there might be one way we can find out pretty quick," Clint said.

"How is that?"

"We can dangle a little bait."

"Bait?" she asked. "What kind of bait?"

"The live kind," he said. "Me."

"I don't understand."

"Well, I'll be asking a lot of questions around town. Maybe the killer will start to worry."

"And you think the killer will try to kill you as well?" she asked.

"She might."

"Yes," Nancy said, "and she might succeed too."

Clint smiled and said, "We'll just have to see to it that she doesn't, won't we?"

THIRTY-THREE

Clint spent the remainder of the day speaking to the other women in town, asking them many of the same questions he had asked the others earlier. Some of them lived in pairs, and in one case there were three women who shared a place, so he was at least able to eliminate some of them as suspects. In fact, he was able to cross more than half of them off his mental list. In the end he was left with Donna Murray, Nancy Peeples, Margaret Colin, her daughter Nia, Jan Grape, Barbara Petty, Ori Hardy, Belle, and one or two other women met just that day whom he really didn't suspect.

Five of the Seven, plus Margaret and Nia, and Belle.

Clint went back to the hotel and saw Belle standing behind the desk. He wondered what she did all day, since no one was staying in the hotel but him.

"There you are," Belle said.

"You been looking for me?"

"You been asking questions all over town," Belle said. "I was wonderin' when you'd get around to me.

He smiled at the big woman as he reached the desk and said, "I guess I was saving the best for last."

"You got that right, sweetie," she said, leaning on the desk. She wasn't wearing the blouse today, but he could see her breasts swell against the fabric of her high-necked dress. "Wanna ask me questions upstairs, in your room?"

"Don't tempt me, Belle."

"Come on," she said, taking hold of his wrist, "take a chance. Maybe it *won't* kill you."

Clint didn't answer. He was staring down at the hold she had on his wrist. Belle was *powerful*. She looked big, almost *fat*, easy to disregard as a comical big woman, but he had never imagined she'd be so strong.

She looked down at his wrist and released the hold she had on him.

"Sorry," she said. "Sometimes I don't know my own strength."

"It's all right," he said. He resisted the urge to rub his wrist. "I think I can ask you the questions down here, Belle."

She looked disappointed and said, "Oh, all right. Go ahead and ask."

He asked her all the same questions, and found out that she *didn't* like Lisa—as he had been told, for the reason he'd been told—and that she did not have an alibi.

"I was in my room alone," she said. "I coulda been in *your* room, and then *neither* one of us woulda been alone—but you already had company, didn't you?"

"I don't know what you mean."

"Sure you do," she said. "I saw Nia come down from your room."

"Well, if you saw her come down you know that we didn't have much time to do anything," he said. "All I did was tell her to get dressed and leave."

"Sure, mister," she said. "A pretty little thing like her and you kicked her out of bed, huh? Just once I'd like the *chance* to get kicked out of bed." Her last statement was said with a certain amount of restrained vehemence. It made Clint frown. How long had this big woman been restraining that vehemence?

"I'll see you later, Belle," he said.

"Sure."

He left the hotel and walked down to the cafe to meet with Nancy. He wanted to talk to her about Belle.

"You suspect Belle?" Nancy asked in disbelief.

"I suspect *everyone*, Nancy," he said. "All I'm saying is that she has a lot of anger pent up inside of her, and she's very *strong*—strong enough to have hit Lisa over the head and then strangle her with a rope."

"How strong do you have to be to strangle an unconscious person with a rope?"

"Not very," he admitted, "but the bump on Lisa's head . . . it wasn't like the sort of bump you get when you hit your head on something, or when *someone* hits you with a gun. It was more . . ."

"More what?"

"Well . . . I'm not an expert, but it was more like someone had hit her in the head with their *fist*."

"A fist?"

"And who in town is that strong?"

"No one," she said. "I mean, *Lisa* was strong, and Belle is probably the strongest woman in town."

"Hey," Clint said, remembering the lock she had put on his wrist, "she just might be the strongest *person* in town right now."

"Belle . . ." Nancy said, shaking her head. "I mean, I know Lisa teased her . . . but I just can't see Belle as someone violent."

"I can."

Nancy looked at him.

"She's been making comments since I've been here—you know, about coming to my bed? I've been putting her off, you know, kidding with her? But today . . . today I saw what must be going on inside of her. The anger, the resentment that's probably built up over the years."

"Yes, but if Belle is the killer, what was it that pushed her over the edge?" Nancy asked.

"I don't know," Clint said. "That's something we'd have to find out."

"Well, there's one thing you better think about," Nancy said.

"What?"

"She's got keys to all the rooms in that hotel—including yours."

"Yeah," Clint said, "I thought about that already."

Their dinner was over and they stood up to leave.

"What do you want to do now?" she asked.

"Well, I *was* thinking about going back to the hotel, just to do a little thinking, but . . ."

"How about my place?" Nancy asked. The request came casually enough. "I mean, I could make some coffee and you could think there."

He stared at her for a moment, then said, "Sure, why not? Thanks."

As Clint and Nancy left the cafe the woman across the street watched them to see which way they were going to go. When they headed east she followed from a distance. The man and woman were too wrapped up in each other to notice she was there. Soon, it became apparent that they were going to Nancy's house.

The woman stopped following.

THIRTY-FOUR

Nancy had taken as her home a small house at the east edge of town, on the Missouri side.

"It's sort of isolated," she said. "Most of the others chose to live more towards the center of town."

They went inside, and Clint saw that it was a nice little three-room house. It had a bedroom, a kitchen, and a parlor or living room.

"I'll make coffee," she said. "Make yourself at home."

He sat down on the sofa in the parlor and looked around. There were some pictures on the walls, but he thought that they had probably already been there when Nancy moved in.

He was thinking about the interviews he'd conducted that day when she entered carrying a tray with a coffeepot and two cups on it. She set it down on the table in front of the sofa, poured two cups, and handed him one. She took hers and sat at the other end of the sofa.

"Tell me about this town," he said.

"What do you want to know?"

"Well, you certainly didn't build it."

"Oh, no, it was here," she said. "You see, Lisa and I both lived in Missouri, and we knew about this town. It used to be called Elkin, and it had been deserted for a

139

long time. A ghost town, actually. When we started to get the idea for . . . for Freedom, we thought about this place. We rode out here together one day, looked at it, and decided that this was where we were going to live."

"Were either of you . . . married, at that point?" he asked.

She looked away and sipped her coffee.

"I'm sorry," he said. "That was a personal question. It's really none of my business."

"No, I'll answer it," she said. "I was married to a man for five years. The first year of our marriage was idyllic—but the last four . . . well, he became more and more *physically* abusive, until I couldn't take it any longer."

"What did you do? Leave him?"

"I tried," she said, "but he came after me and brought me back to him—dragged me, actually."

"What did you do?"

"I did the only thing I could do," she said. The statement hung in the air for a few moments, and then she said, "I killed him."

He didn't know what to say to that. Should he ask how? Did that matter? He decided not to ask, but then she told him anyway.

"I killed him while he was asleep," she said. Her voice shook, as did her hands. The cup clattered against the saucer until she put them both down on the table. "I—I wanted to make damned sure that I succeeded the first time, because if I didn't I felt sure that he would kill me. I felt *sure* that he was going to kill me eventually anyway, so this was my only way out."

She paused, as if playing it over in her mind, and he kept quiet, not wanting to break the spell she seemed to be under.

"So, while he slept," she said, "I took his gun, placed it against the side of his head . . . here"—she touched her left temple—"and pulled the trigger."

She sat there, staring silently ahead, but she wasn't looking at anything in the house. She was looking at something *she* could see and *he* couldn't.

"I didn't know what to expect. I certainly *didn't* expect that his . . . *brains* would come out the other side of the head. I think I thought that the bullet would go in and kill him, but that nothing would come *out*."

"What did you do?"

"I ran away," she said. "I went to Lisa's, and we came here. The law is probably still looking for me . . . back there."

"You did what you felt you had to do, Nancy," he said.

"Sure," she said, looking at him. "Sure, it's always easy to justify something by saying that . . . like the robberies . . ."

"Uh, Nancy," he said, putting down his cup and holding up his hand, "you might not want to say anything more on *that* subject . . ."

"I'd like to . . . if it's all right with you?" she said.

"Sure," he said, and then thought, *Go ahead and add to my moral dilemma.* "Go ahead."

"I'm not really sure whose idea it was at first," she said. "We realized pretty soon that the more women we added to our population, the more money we were going to need. It might have been me, or Lisa, or both who came up with the idea for the robberies.

"At the time it was a thing to do. We needed the money and there was no other way to get it. We *swore* that we'd pull the robberies without hurting anyone. Lisa and I went on the first one, because we couldn't ask anyone to do something we wouldn't do ourselves. It seemed only fair . . .

"So . . . we did the first one, and after that we started drawing straws. The only people who have never gone on a robbery are Margaret, Nia, and Belle. Margaret because we'd need her if one of *us* came back hurt, Nia because she was too young, and Belle because— well, she's just too big to go unnoticed."

"Did Belle ever want to go?"

"Oh, yes," Nancy said, "in the beginning, but after we explained it to her . . ." She trailed off, and Clint knew that she'd thought of something else.

"Who explained it to her, Nancy?" he asked.

"Uh . . . Lisa," she said.

"How?"

"She, uh, told Belle she was too big and fat to sit a horse," Nancy said. "I mean, she was *kidding* . . ."

"Was she?"

"Well . . . I thought so at the time."

They had more coffee, and then Nancy went into the kitchen to make some more.

Later, he asked, "Don't you have some work I'm keeping you from?"

"Well, I *do* have to go over the amount of money the last two robberies brought in, and then allot it to the girls. We *all* get some of it . . . but you don't want to hear about that."

"Hey," he said, "I've heard too much already for you to let me live."

She looked at him sharply and he said, "Sorry, it was a bad joke. Look, I can leave while you do what you have to do."

"No," she said, "stay. I can do it in the kitchen. Afterward I can make a little snack, or something. I think I've got some pie."

"Sure," he said, "fine."

It was at that point that he knew they were going to end up in her bed.

Later, she told him she knew it long before that.

THIRTY-FIVE

Nancy Peeples had an amazing body. There was not an ounce of fat on her. Her shoulders were wide-set, her breasts small but solid, her arms well-toned, her waist slim, her legs slender but powerful. If she were an animal she would have been a racehorse for certain. She was amazingly athletic, and demonstrated that fact in her bed.

They did not end up in her bed until after he had sampled a piece of her apple pie. When they finished they stared at each other across the table. She stood up then and reached for his plate, but instead he took her hand and drew her close to him. He leaned over to kiss her, and at first contact of their lips she drew back. She did this three times. She did not move away from him, simply jerked her head a bit, moving her lips away from him as if he were giving her some sort of shock. Finally, the fourth time she did not draw away and he kissed her, gently at first, then more firmly. She pressed her lips to his then, and he drew her even closer, until the length of her was pressed firmly to him.

After the kiss she took his hand and led him to her bedroom . . .

• • •

In bed she was ravenous, covering his body with kisses before she centered her attention on his solid penis. She held it, spoke to it, licked it, and finally drew it into her mouth hungrily. She sucked it aggressively, fondling his balls, squeezing them ever so slightly, and when he exploded into her mouth she groaned and sucked harder . . .

Later, he slid between her legs and she lifted her knees so high that they ended up hooked over his shoulders. He slammed into her that way, while she exhorted him on by whispering, "Harder . . . harder . . ." no matter how hard he was already doing it . . .

Still later, she got on her hands and knees and he knelt behind her and entered her that way. She gripped the headboard tightly and drove her taut buttocks back against him every time he thrust his hips forward. She felt so tight that being inside of her was like a fist pulling on him, trying to *yank* an explosion out of him . . .

They lay side by side, perspiration drying on their bodies, and Nancy said, "I knew men had their uses, but I'd forgotten what they were."

He placed his hand on her taut belly and just left it there. She caught her breath, then started to breathe again, deeply.

"Jesus," she said, "I feel like I've been dead for a long time, and you've brought me back to life."

"Believe me," he said, "you're not dead."

"No," she said, "I'm not . . . I don't think any of us are. You know," she said, and he could tell from the sound of her voice that she had turned her face towards him, "I've been thinking lately that this . . . Freedom, I mean . . . is all wrong, and now I know it."

"Being with me made you realize it?" he said. "I'm flattered."

"Yes, of course being with you was part of it," she said, "but I think I've known it for a long time—and I think Lisa *knew* I was thinking that."

"And she didn't agree," he said.

"Right."

"She was afraid that you would change things."

"Yes."

"And that's why she wanted to replace you."

"That's right," she said. "Does that make me more of a suspect in her murder?"

"On the contrary," he said. "Everything you've just said gave *her* motives to kill *you*, and not the other way around."

Nancy moved into the circle of Clint's arm, and soon her easy breathing signaled that she had fallen asleep.

What if, he thought, Nancy *knew* that Lisa was going to try to kill her, and instead killed Lisa first? She could certainly have used the same justification she had used for killing her husband, that she was acting in self-defense. Actually, the killing of her husband was self-*preservation* more than self-defense.

No, Clint didn't think that Nancy had killed Lisa. In fact, he was sure of only two people in town being innocent, Nancy and Kate.

The more he thought about it, the better Belle looked for it.

Poor Belle, he thought. Even though he suspected her of killing Lisa, it was Belle he felt sorry for, and not Lisa.

Wasn't that odd?

THIRTY-SIX

In the morning they left Nancy's house together. Clint was glad that Nancy had picked such an isolated part of town to live in. It kept anyone from *seeing* them leave together, which might have caused some trouble for Nancy.

"I know what you're thinking," Nancy said as they walked towards the center of town.

"One night together and you already think you can read my mind?"

"You tell me if I'm wrong."

"All right," he said, "go ahead."

"You're glad no one saw us come out of my house together," she said. "You think that would cause me trouble."

"You're amazing."

"Actually," she said, "it wouldn't cause me any trouble. After this is all over, and we've found Lisa's killer, I'm going to suggest that we turn Freedom over to the ghosts again."

"And if there are women who want to stay?"

"That's fine too," she said, "but I'm not staying."

"Where are you going to go?"

"I don't know," she said. "Maybe I'll go back and face up to killing my husband. After that, I can get on with my life again."

"Maybe you should just go someplace where nobody knows you and start over," he said. "From what you told me about your husband, I don't think you have anything to face up to."

"Maybe not," she said. "I'll think it over. Of course, there are all the robberies . . ."

"Forget about them."

"Can *you*?" she asked.

"Sure," he said, "why not?"

"Come on," she said. "Don't you feel some sort of obligation to turn us in?"

He thought about it a moment, and then said, "No, I don't. If you had been doing it just to do it—I mean, if you were all *real* outlaw women—it would be different."

"Outlaw women," Nancy said, tasting the phrase. "A whole town full of outlaw women, that's what we are."

"Maybe not anymore," he said, "if they listen to you."

"Some of them will," she said, "and some of them will probably try to keep it going, but I think the idea is dead, Clint. I think it failed, and was doomed to fail right from the beginning. We can't hide from the rest of the world. It just can't be done. I've learned that, and now I'll see if I can teach it to the others."

"It might be hard," he said. "After all, it was you—you and Lisa—who brought them here."

"And soon," she said, "we'll both be gone. That in itself should tell the others that the idea just didn't work."

As they approached the center of town they saw that many of the women were assembled there, milling about.

"Something's wrong," Nancy said, and broke into a trot. Clint continued to walk, allowing Nancy to reach the group first and find out what was wrong.

When he reached them she turned to him and said, "It's happened again."

"What?" he said. "Who?"

"Vicky," Nancy said. "Vicky's dead."

THIRTY-SEVEN

Of course, it was wrong of Clint to feel guilt over Vicky's death. If he *hadn't* slept with Nancy, if he had *instead* gone to be with Vicky, she would probably still be alive. He knew that, and he felt guilty about it, in spite of what Nancy said.

"Don't feel guilty," Nancy said. "Please. It's not your fault."

"I know it's not my fault," he said. "But still . . ."

They were in the meeting room in the town hall, waiting for the other members of the Seven to arrive. They filed in one by one, with Donna Murray the last to come in. Her eyes were red-rimmed from crying. She too felt guilty. If she hadn't left Vicky alone . . .

"All right," Kate said loudly—perhaps *too* loudly, "it's happened again. Now will you believe me? He's done it again. He's killed another one of us."

They all looked at Clint, but before he could say anything it was Nancy who spoke.

"Clint didn't kill Vicky."

"Who says?" Kate asked.

"*I* do," she said. She looked at all of the others and said, "He was with me."

"All night?" Kate said.

"Yes," Nancy said, "all night."

"Nancy . . ." Jan said, shaking her head. The others didn't say anything.

"All right," Ori Hardy said, "so it wasn't him, and he probably didn't kill Lisa either. So who did?"

Nancy and Clint exchanged a glance, but he decided not to mention his suspicions about Belle. At least, not until he could think about this new murder. What could Belle have had against Vicky? What could *anyone* have had against Vicky? She was not as aggressive or abrasive as Lisa had been, and she was in no position of authority.

"This makes even less sense than Lisa's death," Donna Murray said. "Why would anyone kill Vicky?"

Nancy was seated closest to Donna, and reached out to take her hand. Donna held onto Nancy's hand tightly.

"What do we do now?" Kate asked. Learning that Clint had been with Nancy all night seemed to have taken the wind out of her sails. She sat down heavily and stared straight ahead of her.

"Did anyone hear anything or see anything last night?" Clint asked.

They all said they hadn't.

"Was everyone alone?"

They all said they were.

"I went back to my own place," Donna said. "Vicky insisted on it. She said—she said I had already spent too much time with her."

"We're back where we started from then," Clint said. "We don't know who, or why."

"I have something to say," Nancy said, and all eyes turned to her. "I think we should leave."

"What?" Jan said.

"I think we should leave here before someone else gets killed," Nancy said. "I mean, it's clear that someone killed Lisa and Vicky, and they may kill someone else. If we *leave*, that won't happen."

"You mean . . . give up Freedom?" Ori Hardy asked.

"Yes," Nancy said. "Give it up, give it all up. It didn't work, I think we all know that, and before someone else gets killed—"

"If we do that," Kate said, "the killer will get away with it."

"Perhaps," Nancy said, "but no one else will get killed."

"I don't want that," Kate said. "I want the killer to pay."

"I agree with Kate," Donna Murray said. "I want to know who the killer is."

"Wait a minute," Barbara Petty said. "I agree with Nancy. Let's get out of here before someone else— maybe one of *us*—gets killed."

They all started talking at once then, each trying to be heard over the other.

"Settle down!" Clint shouted, and he banged his palm down on the table to get their attention, which he did.

"I think you all should make up your own minds about this," he said. "Gather all of the women in town together, explain it to them, and then let the ones who want to leave go ahead and leave, and the ones who don't want to leave can stay."

"What will the killer do?" Kate wondered out loud.

"There's no way we can know that," Clint said. "I think maybe the *killer* doesn't even know what she's going to do next."

"What do you mean?" Ori asked.

"I mean I think the killer is a demented woman. Why else would she have killed Vicky? What could she possibly have had against Vicky? What did Vicky have that no one else did?"

There was silence, and then Donna said, "You."

"What?" Clint said.

"Vicky and you . . . on the trail . . . she told me about it," Donna said. "That's what she had that none of us have had . . . except for Nancy now."

"You think Vicky was killed because she slept with Clint?" Nancy said.

"If that's so," Kate said, "why was Lisa killed?"

"Because of him," Barbara said, getting into the spirit of things now.

"I don't understand," Nancy said.

"Don't you see?" Donna said. "Lisa wanted to kill Clint, so somebody killed her."

"And Vicky *slept* with him, so the killer killed her too," Barbara said.

"That doesn't make sense," Nancy said.

"Sure it does," Jan said. "On one hand the killer was protecting him, and on the other hand she was . . . hurting him?"

"Getting revenge against Vicky for sleeping with him?" Barbara said.

"Why? Because the *killer* hasn't slept with him?" Kate asked.

"Wait a minute," Clint said. "This is all very flattering, but—"

"No," Nancy said, "it makes sense . . . sort of. *First* the killer wanted to protect you, so she killed Lisa. That way she kept you alive, and had a chance to be with you herself." She looked at him and asked, "Have you slept with anyone . . . anyone *else* besides me since you've been here?"

"No," he said, "of course not."

"What about Nia?" Nancy asked.

"What about Nia?" Jan asked. Jan and Margaret Colin were good friends.

"Nia was in his room," Nancy said.

"What was Nia doing in your room?" Jan demanded.

"She wanted to sleep with me," Clint said. "I made her get dressed and leave."

Jan eyed him suspiciously.

"I think we have to believe him at this point," Nancy said. "So, you haven't slept with anyone, and then last night you slept with me."

"So," Barbara said, taking up the train of thought, "the killer saw him with you and got angry."

"And killed Vicky?" Donna asked.

"Sure," Ori said, "because Vicky has slept with him, and the killer hasn't."

They all exchanged glances and it seemed to make sense to all of the women. Clint was still slightly baffled by the whole line of . . . logic?

"If that's the case," Nancy said, "then I would be next."

"What about Nia?" Jan asked, suddenly.

"I told you I didn't sleep with Nia," Clint said plaintively.

"Maybe," Nancy said, "but does the killer know that?" She looked around and asked, "Has anyone seen Nia today?"

THIRTY-EIGHT

They all left the town hall then and started running down towards Margaret Colin's office. There were still women in the streets, just sort of walking aimlessly. Most of them were still in shock over the events of the past few days. When they came to live in the town called Freedom, they had never expected murder to intrude on their lives.

Clint ran fastest of all, followed closely by the athletic Nancy, with Kate close on *her* heels. The others were left far back.

Clint reached the door, tried it, and found it locked. As Nancy and Kate reached him he kicked out at the door, snapping it open. It had never occurred to him to try knocking.

"Margaret!" Nancy shouted.

"Maggie?" Kate called.

Clint entered her examination room and found the woman lying on the floor. As he bent over her Nancy and Kate entered. Behind them the others were only just entering.

"Is she dead?" Nancy asked.

"No," Clint said, "she's just unconscious."

He lifted her in his arms and put her on the examination table. There was a bruise on her right cheekbone—a very recent bruise.

"This happened today," he said, touching her face, "this morning."

"Maggie," Nancy said.

Kate appeared with a damp cloth, and they applied it to Margaret's face. Jan crowded near the table, but the others stayed back.

When Margaret Colin's eyes fluttered open they all breathed a sigh of relief—but it was short-lived.

"Where's Nia?" Margaret asked right away.

"We don't know, Maggie," Kate said. "What happened here?"

"She—she was crazy!" Margaret said. "She came in here like a madwoman, shouting for Nia. I tried to stop her—tried to hide Nia, but she grabbed her and—and then she hit me."

"Who, Maggie?" Clint said. "Who are you talking about. Belle?"

"Yes," Margaret said, "yes, Belle. She's crazy! She has Nia."

Clint turned and looked at Nancy.

"Belle?" Jan Grape said. "Belle killed Lisa?"

"And Vicky?" Donna asked.

"Oh, my God," Margaret said, "and now she's got Nia."

Clint turned to all the women and said, "All right, we've got to find her. She may not have harmed Nia yet. Think! Where would she go?"

"Where else?" Nancy said. "The hotel. When she first arrived here Belle said she wanted the hotel. No one else wanted it, so she took it. She hardly ever *leaves* it."

"Let's go!" Kate said. It did not escape Clint's notice

that the tiny blonde was still wearing Lisa Ford's gunbelt.

"No!" he said aloud. "I'll go alone."

"Why?" Kate demanded.

"If too many of us go she might hurt Nia," Clint said. "And if the logic you've all assailed me with this morning is true, then Belle will want to talk to me."

"What's going on?" Margaret demanded. "Why is this happening?"

Clint looked at Nancy and said, "Explain it to her. I'll go to the hotel."

At that moment another woman entered the room and said, "Nancy! You better come quick."

"What's wrong, Leila?"

The woman called Leila said, "Men, lots of them. They're just outside of town."

"Missouri side or Kansas?" Kate asked.

"Kansas," Leila said.

Kate looked at Clint and Nancy and said, "Damn, a posse."

"They must have tracked the robbers here," Nancy said.

"What do we do?" Kate asked.

"They don't know anything," Clint said. "They can't. They're just looking."

"But why have they come this far?" Nancy asked. "No one was killed—"

"Never mind," Clint said, cutting her off. "Nancy, Kate, get everyone off the street. When the posse rides in talk to them, just the two of you. Kate . . ."

"Yes?"

"Leave that gun inside."

"But—"

"But nothing," he said. "If you're wearing that gun it's

going to look odd to them. It might make them start to think. You two have got to handle the posse. I've got to see to Belle."

"All right," Kate said, and unbuckled the gun.

"Shouldn't you handle the posse, Clint?" Nancy asked him.

"No," he said, "they'll be less threatened by you. Just don't *say* anything about the robberies. Don't admit to anything, Nancy. Understand?"

"I understand."

"There are more lives at stake than just yours."

"I *understand!*" she said.

"Good. All of you, get out there and get the rest of the women off the street, and keep them off until the posse is gone and we're finished with Belle. Let's move!"

THIRTY-NINE

They left Margaret's place together, spreading out as they reached the street. Donna, Barbara, and the others started urging people to get off the street. Nancy walked with Margaret and Kate, obviously explaining to Margaret about Belle. Clint headed for the hotel, hoping that Belle had indeed taken Nia there.

He still found it difficult to believe that Belle might have killed Lisa and Vicky, *and* taken Nia, because of him. If that was the case, then he was probably just the catalyst for something that had been buried inside her for years and years. Perhaps, if he had never come to Freedom, it would have lain dormant for years to come, or forever. Or maybe she would have gone on a killing spree anyway.

Jesus, he just remembered that he hadn't even asked *how* Vicky was killed.

People were running in the streets now, hopefully heading for their homes. He broke into a run, and only slowed when he reached the hotel. He hoped Nancy and Kate could handle the posse, then took a deep breath and entered the hotel.

• • •

Nancy explained the situation to Margaret, and then the nurse went with Jan, who would take her off the street. Kate and Nancy stayed together while the other members of the Seven cleared the streets.

"I'm scared," Kathleen Dougherty said to Nancy.

"So am I, Kate," Nancy said. "We can do this, though. It's like Clint said. They can't know that we committed those robberies. They're probably just stopping to ask questions and get supplies."

Kate looked over her shoulder and said, "I wonder how Clint's doing."

"He's doing what he can," Nancy said. "We have to do the same."

They stood together, waiting for the posse to ride into town.

Clint entered the hotel lobby slowly, carefully, looking around. Belle was not behind the desk, but he remembered her telling him that she lived in the back. There was a curtained doorway in the wall right behind the desk. He walked to the desk, went around it, and through the curtain.

He found himself in a hallway. Down at the end was a door, and there was a door on the left and two on the right. He recognized the hall. He had entered from a different direction last time, but this was where he had come for his bath. The door on the left, then, led to the bathroom. The door at the end of the hall probably led to the outside, behind the hotel. That meant that one of the doors on the right led to Belle's room. Where did the other one lead? That really didn't matter now.

He decided to let Belle know he was there.

"Belle?" he called.

No answer.

"Belle? It's Clint. I'm here."

Still no answer.

"Belle, let Nia go. She hasn't done anything."

He waited a moment, and was about to call out again when a door opened and Belle stepped out. She was so much taller and bigger than Nia that she simply held the young girl by the hair with one hand. She was pulling up so hard on her hair that Nia's chin almost pointed to the ceiling and she was standing on her toes.

"Belle," he said.

"Now you'd go to bed with me if I asked," Belle said, "wouldn't ya?"

The posse appeared at the end of the street. Nancy counted eight riders. She felt Kate stiffen next to her, and briefly touched the smaller woman's hand. The posse rode up to them and stopped. The lead rider was wearing a badge.

"Mornin', ladies," he said, touching his hat.

"Sheriff," she said. "What can I do for you?"

"Ain't this the town of Elkin?"

"It used to be," she said.

"I heard this was a ghost town."

"It used to be," she said again.

"You ladies here alone?"

"There are others," Nancy said.

"You live here?"

"We do."

"What do you call the place?"

Nancy hesitated, then said, "Freedom."

"Freedom?" he asked, surprised.

A man behind him said, "Ain't that a helluva name for a town, Clem?"

Nancy couldn't tell which of the men was Clem.

The sheriff looked around, then looked back at Nancy and Kate. Behind him the men were craning their necks to get a look at both of the attractive women.

"Still looks like a ghost town," the sheriff said. "Many of you, are there?"

"No," Nancy said, "not many."

"Well, ma'am," the sheriff said, "we're lookin' for some bank robbers. You wouldn't happen to know anythin' about that, would you?"

"No, Sheriff," Nancy said, "we wouldn't know anything about that at all."

"Belle," Clint said, "take it easy. We know what you've done."

"What have I done?"

"You killed Lisa, and Vicky."

"Lisa was a bitch," Belle said. "Always teasing me about bein' fat just because she was so beautiful. Well, I'll bet that *somewhere* in the world there's a man who woulda thought *I* was the beautiful one."

"I'm sure there is, Belle."

"Sure . . ."

"Why did you kill Vicky, Belle?" Clint asked. "What did she do to you?"

"You slept with Vicky, didn't you?" Belle asked. "I heard some of the women talkin', saying you slept with Vicky on the trail—and then last night I saw you go with Nancy. You went to her house and you slept with *her*."

"So you killed *Vicky?*" he said. "Because you thought I slept with Nancy? Belle . . . what kind of sense did that make?"

"Vicky slept with you," Belle said, "Nancy slept with you, *Nia* slept with you—"

"I didn't—" Nia said, but Belle yanked on her hair and said, "Shut up!"

"She didn't sleep with me, Belle," Clint said. "I told you that."

"Sure," Belle said, "I'm gonna believe you, you with your smiles and your sweet talk. I thought you *liked* me. Were you gonna sleep with *everyone* in town but me? Was that it? Make fun of me like that?"

"Belle—"

"See her?" Belle said, yanking Nia by the hair again. "See your little girlfriend? Watch me, 'cause I'm gonna snap her neck like a twig. I'm *strong*. I can *do it*."

"I know you can, Belle," Clint said. "I know you can, but I'm asking you not to."

"You don't want me to kill her, huh?"

"No, I don't."

"Okay then," Belle said, "you give me one reason why I shouldn't—just *one*—and I won't."

Clint licked his lips. He knew that Nia's life depended on what he said next.

FORTY

"Belle," he said, "Belle . . . don't kill her."

Oh, good, Adams, he told himself, that's *damned* convincing.

"Belle . . . she's just a child, you can't possibly think I would have slept with her."

"A child, eh?" Belle said. She held Nia tightly by the hair with her left hand. With her right she reached down, yanked Nia's shirt from her pants, and pulled it up, revealing her small, solid breasts.

"Does this look like the body of a child?" Belle demanded. "She doesn't even wear *underwear!*"

"Belle—"

"Do you know what *I* would give to have a body like this?" Belle asked. Her hand moved over the girl's breasts, but Clint doubted she knew what she was doing.

"Are you going to tell me you didn't want *this* body?" Belle demanded, roughly squeezing Nia's breasts now.

"Belle . . . she's a child, Belle . . . and you're a woman."

"Are you telling me you'd prefer me to *her?*" Belle demanded.

"Given a choice between you and her," Clint said,

"the answer is yes, Belle. Yes, I'd prefer you."

"Then prove it."

He spread his hands out and asked, "How?"

"Make love to me," Belle said. "Sleep with me and I won't kill her."

"All right," he said, "all right, Belle . . . where?"

"In there," Belle said, pointing to the room they had just come out of. "Will you do it?"

"Yes."

"Why don't you just shoot me? I don't have a gun, or a weapon. Why don't you just shoot me?"

He didn't want to fire because of the posse outside, but he didn't want to tell her that.

"Belle," he said, "why should I shoot you when I could make love to you?"

"Then come ahead," Belle said. She backed away from the open door, draggng Nia by the hair with her. "Come ahead, Clint Adams, and let's see what kind of a man you are."

"No strangers have come to town at all?" the sheriff asked.

"None, Sheriff," Nancy said. "Like you said, most people think this is a ghost town."

"And we like it that way," Kate added.

"Is that so?" the lawman said.

"Yes."

He looked around again and said, "I don't see any men."

"I don't see *anybody*, Clem," the man behind him said. Nancy finally decided that the sheriff must be Clem.

"No," Clem the sheriff said, "me neither. We might as well head back. This was our last hope in Kansas, and we can't go into Missouri."

Nancy wondered if she should tell the sheriff that *he* was already a few feet inside Missouri while the rest of his posse was still in Kansas.

"Can we offer you anything?" she asked. "Supplies?"

"No, thanks, ma'am," the sheriff said. "We're travelin' light. Thanks for your help."

"Sure, Sheriff," she said. "Anytime."

"Let's go, boys," the lawman said. He turned his posse around, and they rode back out the way they had come.

"Jesus . . ." Nancy said, feeling drained.

"Let's see how Clint's doing," Kate said.

They turned and ran towards the hotel.

"Come on," Belle said. "Go inside. I'll let her go and come in with you."

"Please—" Nia said.

"Shut up!" Belle said, shaking her by the hair. "Just shut up!"

Once he was in the room with her and Nia was free, Clint wasn't sure what he would do. He certainly couldn't have sex with the woman. Oh, under normal circumstances he guessed he could have, but he doubted that he could perform under *these* conditions. Maybe, once they were in her room, he could subdue her. Remembering her strength, he wondered if he could do it without his gun.

"I'm coming, Belle," he said. "Take it easy. I'm coming."

He started down the hall slowly, and had almost reached the door when he heard Nancy call out from the lobby, "Clint?"

Shit, he said to himself.

"Who's that?" Belle asked, pulling on Nia's hair. She yanked the girl's hair so hard that Nia couldn't help but scream.

From behind the curtain Nancy and Kate appeared in the hall.

"Get away!" Belle screamed, spittle flying from her mouth. "Get away or I'll kill her!"

Clint was only a few feet from her and he made his move. He charged her, one hand held straight out in front of him. He rammed her in the face with his hand and, startled, she released Nia's hair. The young girl reacted instantly, sprinting away from the big woman.

Belle was too fast for Clint, though. She recovered, reached out, and grabbed *his* arm in a hold that was like a vise. He tried to break free, bracing his legs and pulling, but she was too strong.

"Now!" she said, and he didn't know what she meant to do. She was pulling him *to* her.

It was clear that he couldn't match her amazing strength, but he had to try. He did the only thing he could think to do. He balled up his fist and punched her flush in the face.

Belle blinked, shook her head, and then growled deep in her throat. The punch had split her bottom lip, but other than that had had no discernible effect on her.

"Shit," he said.

Bad idea.

"I'll kill you!" she screamed, spraying spittle and blood.

"Clint?" Nancy called.

Kate cursed, wishing she had Lisa's gun.

Nia had reached Nancy and Kate and was hiding behind them.

Clint knew that with her strength she probably *could* kill him, and quickly.

He drew his gun, and used it.

FORTY-ONE

"I really thought you were going to shoot her," Nancy said. "I was surprised when you *hit* her with the gun."

"I was surprised when I hit her with my fist and it didn't bother her," he said, "and *then* when I hit her with the gun the first time and she didn't go down."

"She fell when you hit her the second time, though," Nancy said. "She hit the ground like a sack of *flour*."

Clint looked down the street at all of the women who were loading horses and wagons. Walking towards Clint and Nancy were Donna Murray and Kate Dougherty. Clint wished he'd had more time to appreciate how attractive both women were, in such different ways.

"I wanted to apologize," Kate said to him.

"For what?"

"For the way I acted," she said, "for the way I treated you."

"You believed I had killed your friend," Clint said. "You have nothing to apologize for, Kate."

"Well . . . I'm apologizing anyway."

"All right," he said. "Then I accept."

She reached for him, so he bent and let her kiss him.

"Good luck," he said to her.

"You too."

Donna approached him next.

"I think I should apologize too," Donna said. "Vicky told me how you made her feel. You saved her life, and made her *happy*. She wasn't happy here—I think a lot of us weren't happy here, but didn't want to admit it."

"I hope you find that happiness somewhere else," he said.

"I think I will," she said. She kissed him good-bye and walked back to the others, leaving him with Nancy.

"What are you going to do with Belle?" Clint asked.

"We can't just let her go," Nancy said. "She might kill someone else."

"She's not vicious," Clint said, "just funny in the head. She needs medical help."

"Then we'll try and see that she gets it," Nancy said.

"Where are you going to go, Nancy?" he asked.

"Back, I think."

"To face up to the law for killing your husband?"

"Yes," she said. "Kate's going to come with me. We'll take Belle there too."

"What about the robberies," he said. "You're not going to own up to all the robberies, are you?"

"No," she said, "there were too many of us involved in those. I'm just going to face up to my own personal problems. I'll let the others take care of themselves."

Clint looked up the street again. Within a matter of hours Freedom—or Elkin—would be a ghost town again, and all these women would be coming out of hiding.

"Thank you, Clint," Nancy said.

"For what?"

"Your arrival in town seems to have been the catalyst for a lot of things," she said.

"Sure," he said, "like murder."

"That wasn't your fault," Nancy said. "You said it yourself, Belle is a bit crazy."

"Yeah, I guess so."

"I meant that your arrival made me start to think hard about what I had started here, and made me realize that since I had started it, I had to stop it."

"I just wish you wouldn't go back, Nancy," he said. "Go somewhere else."

"I'd still be hiding."

"But the law's not infallible, you know," he said. "You killed your husband, and you ran. *I* don't think you deserve to go to prison, but you might. You realize that, don't you?"

"Yes, Clint," she said, "I realize that."

She kissed him good-bye then, a long, sweet kiss.

"You're a sweet man," she said.

"Good luck, Nancy."

"Think of me," she said.

She walked away and he climbed up onto his rig to leave before the rest of them did. He *would* think of her—and he would think of all of the women who thought they could find some sort of freedom just by living in a town by that name.

I was hurt, though how badly I didn't know. Some three hours earlier I'd been shot, the ball taking me in the left side of the chest about midway up my rib cage. I didn't know if the slug had broken a rib or just passed between two of them as it exited my back. I'd been in Galveston, trying to collect a gambling debt, when, like a fool kid, I'd walked into a setup that I'd ordinarily have seen coming from the top of a tree stump. I was angry that I hadn't collected the debt, I was more than angry that I'd been shot, but I was furious at myself for having been suckered in such a fashion. I figured if it ever got around that Wilson Young had been gotten that easy, all of the old enemies I'd made through the years would start coming out of the woodwork to pick over the carcass.

But, in a way, I was lucky. By rights I should have been killed outright, facing three of them as I had and having nothing to put me on the alert. They'd had guns in their hands by the time I realized it wasn't money I was going to get, but lead.

Now I was rattling along on a train an hour out of Galveston, headed for San Antonio. It had been lucky, me catching that train just as it was pulling out. Except for that, there was an excellent chance that I would have been incarcerated in Galveston and looking at more trouble than I'd been in in a long time. After the shooting I'd managed to get away from the office where the trouble had happened and make my way toward the depot. I'd been wearing a frock coat of a good quality linen when I'd sat down with Phil Sharp to discuss the money he owed me. Because it was a hot day, I took the coat off and laid it over the arm of the chair I was sitting in. When the shooting was over, I grabbed the coat and the little valise I was carrying and ducked and dodged my way through alleyways and side streets. I came up from the border on the train so, of course, I didn't have a horse with me.

But I did have a change of clothes, having expected to be overnight in Galveston. In an alley I took off my bloody shirt, inspected the wound in my chest, and then wrapped the shirt around me, hoping to keep the blood from showing. Then I put on a clean shirt that fortunately was dark and not white like the one I'd been shot in. After that I donned my frock coat, picked up my valise, and made my way to the train station. I did not know if the law was looking for me or not, but I waited until the train was ready to pull out before I boarded it. I had a round-trip ticket so there'd been no need for me to go inside the depot.

I knew I was bleeding, but I didn't know how long it would be before the blood seeped through my makeshift bandage and then through my shirt and finally showed on my coat.

All I knew was that I was hurting and hurting bad and that I was losing blood to the point where I was beginning to feel faint. It was a six-hour ride to San

Antonio, and I was not at all sure I could last that long. Even if the blood didn't seep through enough to call it to someone's attention, I might well pass out. But I didn't have many options. There were few stops between Galveston and San Antonio, it being a kind of a spur line, and what there were would be small towns that most likely wouldn't even have a doctor. I could get off in one and lay up in a hotel until I got better, but that didn't much appeal to me. I wanted to know how bad I was hurt, and the only way I was going to know that was to hang on until I could get to some good medical attention in San Antone.

I was Wilson Young, and in that year of 1896, I was thirty-two years old. For fourteen of those years, beginning when I was not quite fifteen, I had been a robber. I'd robbed banks, I'd robbed money shipments, I'd robbed high-stakes poker games, I'd robbed rich people carrying more cash than they ought to have been, but mostly I'd robbed banks. But then about four years past, I'd left the owlhoot trail and set out to become a citizen that did not constantly have to be on the lookout for the law. Through the years I'd lost a lot of friends and a lot of members of what the newspapers had chosen to call my "gang"—the Texas Bank Robbing Gang in one headline.

I'd even lost a wife, a woman I'd taken out of a whorehouse in the very same town I was now fleeing from. But Marianne hadn't been a whore at heart; she'd just been kind of briefly and unwillingly forced into it in much the same way I'd taken up robbing banks.

I had been making progress in my attempt to achieve a certain amount of respectability. At first I'd set up on the Mexican side of the border, making occasional forays into Texas to sort of test the waters. Then, as a few years passed and certain amounts of money found their way into the proper hands, I was slowly able to make my way around Texas. I had not been given a pardon by the governor, but emissaries of his had indicated that the state of Texas was happy to have no further trouble with Wilson Young and that the past could be forgotten so long as I did nothing to revive it.

And now had come this trouble. The right or wrong of my position would have nothing to do with it. I was still Wilson Young, and if I was in a place where guns were firing and men were being shot, the prevailing attitude was going to be that it was my doing.

So it wasn't only the wound that was troubling me greatly; it was also the worry about the aftermath of what had begun as a peaceful and lawful business trip. If I didn't die from my wound, there was every chance that I would become a wanted man again, and there would go the new life I had built for myself. And not only that life of peace and legality, but also a great deal of money that I had put into a business in Del Rio, Texas, right along the banks of the Rio Grande. Down there, a stone's throw from Mexico, I owned the most high-class saloon and gambling emporium and whorehouse as there was to be found in Texas. I had at first thought to put it on the Mexican side of the river, but the *mordida*, the bribes, that the officials would have taken convinced me to build it in Texas, where the local law was not quite so greedy. But now, if trouble were to come from this shooting, I'd have to be in Mexico, and my business would be in Texas. It might have been only a stone's throw away, but for me, it might just as well have been a thousand miles. And I'd sunk damn near every cent I had in the place.

My side was beginning to hurt worse with every mile. I supposed it was my wound, but the train was rattling around and swaying back and forth like it was running on crooked rails. I was in the last car before the caboose, and every time we rounded a curve, the car would rock back and forth like it was fixing to quit the tracks and take off across the prairie. Fortunately, the train wasn't very crowded and I had a seat to myself. I was sort of sitting in the middle of the double cushion and leaning to my right against the wall of the car. It seemed to make my side rest easier to stretch it out like that. My valise was at my feet, and with a little effort, I bent down and fumbled it open with my right hand. Since my wound had begun to stiffen up, my left arm had become practically useless—to use it would almost put tears in my eyes.

I had a bottle of whiskey in my valise, and I fumbled it out, pulled the cork with my teeth and then had a hard pull. There was a spinsterish middle-aged lady sitting right across the aisle from me, and she give me such a look of disapproval that I thought for a second that she was going to call the conductor and make a commotion. As best I could, I got the cork back in the bottle and then hid it out of sight between my right side and the wall of the car.

Outside, the terrain was rolling past. It was the coastal prairie of south Texas, acres and acres of flat, rolling plains that grew the best grazing grass in the state. It would stay that way until the train switched tracks and turned west for San Antonio. But that was another two hours away. My plan was to get myself fixed up in San Antone and then head out for Del Rio and the Mexican side of the border just as fast as I could. From there I'd try and find out just what sort of trouble I was in.

That was, if I lived that long.

With my right hand I pulled back the left side of my coat, lifting it gently, and looked underneath. I could see just the beginning of a stain on the dark blue shirt I'd changed into. Soon it would soak through my coat and someone would notice it. I had a handkerchief in my pocket, and I got that out and slipped it inside my shirt, just under the stain. I had no way of holding it there, but so long as I kept still, it would stay in place.

Of course I didn't know what was happening at my back. For all I knew the blood had already seeped through and stained my coat. That was all right so long as my back was against the seat, but it would be obvious as soon as I got up. I just had to hope there would be no interested people once I got to San Antone and tried to find a doctor.

I knew the bullet had come out my back. I knew it because I'd felt around and located the exit hole while I'd been hiding in the alley, using one shirt for a bandage and the other for a sop. Of course the hole in my back was bigger than the entrance hole the bullet had made. It was always that way, especially if a bullet hit something hard like a bone and went to tumbling or flattened out. I could have stuck my thumb in the hole in my back.

About the only good thing I could find to feel hopeful about was the angle of the shot. The bullet had gone in very near the bottom of my ribs and about six inches from my left side. But it had come out about only three or four inches from my side. That meant there was a pretty good chance that it had missed most of the vital stuff and such that a body has got inside itself. I knew it hadn't nicked my lungs because I was breathing fine. But there is a whole bunch of other stuff inside a man that a bullet ain't going to do a bit of good. I figured it had cracked a rib for sure because it hurt to breathe deep, but that didn't even necessarily have to be so. It was hurting so bad anyway that I near about couldn't separate the different kinds of hurt.

A more unlikely man than Phil Sharp to give me my seventh gunshot wound I could not have imagined. I had ended my career on the owlhoot trail with my body having lived through six gunshots. That, as far as I was concerned, had been a-plenty. By rights I should have been dead, and there had been times when I had been given up for dead. But once off the outlaw path I'd thought my days of having my blood spilt were over. Six was enough.

And then Phil Sharp had given me my seventh. As a gambler I didn't like the number. There was nothing lucky about it that I could see, and I figured that anything that wasn't lucky had to be unlucky.

Part of my bad luck was because I *was* Wilson Young. Even though I'd been retired for several years, I was still, strictly speaking, a wanted man. And if anybody had cause to take interest in my condition, it might mean law—and law would mean trouble.

For that matter Phil Sharp and the three men he'd had with him might have thought they could shoot me without fear of a murder charge because of the very fact of my past and my uncertain position with regard to the law, both local and through the state. Hell, for all I knew some of those rewards that had been posted on my head might still be lying around waiting for someone to claim them. It hadn't been so many years past that my name and my likeness had been on Wanted posters in every sheriff's office in every county in Texas.

I had gone to see Phil Sharp because he'd left my gambling house owing me better than twenty thousand dollars. I didn't, as an ordinary matter, advance credit at the gaming tables, but Sharp had been a good customer in the past and I knew him to be a well-to-do man. He owned a string of warehouses along the docks in Galveston, which was the biggest port in Texas. The debt had been about a month old when I decided to go and see him. When he'd left Del Rio, he'd promised to wire me the money as soon as he was home, but it had never come. Letters and telegrams jogging his memory had done no good, so I'd decided to call on him in person. It wasn't just the twenty thousand; there was also the matter that it ain't good policy for a man running a casino and cathouse to let word get around that he's careless about money owed him. And in that respect I was still the Wilson Young it was best not to get too chancy with. Sharp knew my reputation and I did not figure to have any trouble with him. If he didn't have the twenty thousand handy, I figured we could come to some sort of agreement as to how he could pay it off. I had wired him before I left Del Rio that I was planning a trip to Houston and was going to look in on him in Galveston. He'd wired back that he'd be expecting me.

I saw him in his office in the front of one of the warehouses he owned down along the waterfront. He was behind his desk when I was shown in, getting up to shake hands with me. He was dressed like he usually was, in an expensive suit with a shiny vest and a big silk tie. Sharp himself was a little round man in his forties with a kind of baby face and a look that promised you could trust him with your virgin sister. Except I'd seen him without the suit and vest, chasing one of my girls down the hall at four o'clock in the morning with a bottle of whiskey in one hand and the handle to his hoe in the other. I'd also seen him at the poker table with sweat pouring off his face as he tried to make a straight beat a full house. It hadn't then and it probably never would.

He acted all surprised that I hadn't gotten my money, claiming he'd mailed it to me no less than a week ago. He said, "I got to apologize for the delay, but I had to use most of my ready cash on some shipments to England. Just let me step in the next room and look at my canceled checks. I'd almost swear I saw it just the other day. Endorsed by you."

Like I said, he looked like a man that might shoot you full of holes in a business deal, but not the sort of man who could use or would use a gun.

He got up from his desk and went to a door at the back, just to my right. I took off my coat and laid it over the arm of the chair, it being warm in the office. I was sitting kind of forward on the chair, feeling a little uneasy for some reason. It was that, but it was mainly the way Sharp opened the back door that probably saved my life. When you're going through a door, you pull it to you and step to your left, toward the opening, so as to pass through. But Sharp pulled open the door and then stepped back. In that instant, I slid out of the chair I was sitting in and down to my knees. As I did, three men with hoods pulled over their heads came through the door with pistols in their hands. Their first volley would have killed me if I'd still been sitting in the chair. But they fired at where I'd been, and by the time they could cock their pistols for another round, I had my revolver in my hand and was firing. They never got off another shot; all three went down under my rapid-fire volley.

Then I became aware that Phil Sharp was still in the room, just by the open door. I was about to swing my revolver around on him when I saw a little gun in his hand. He fired, once, and hit me in the chest. I knew it was a low-caliber gun because the blow of the slug just twitched at my side, not even knocking me off balance.

But it surprised me so that it gave Sharp time to cut through the open door and disappear into the blackness of the warehouse. I fired one shot after him, knowing it was in vain, and then pulled the trigger on an empty chamber.

I had not brought any extra cartridges with me. In the second I stood there with an empty gun, I couldn't remember why I hadn't brought any extras, but the fact was that I was standing there, wounded, with what amounted to a useless piece of iron in my fist. As quick as I could, expecting people to suddenly come bursting in the door, I got over to where the three men were lying on the floor and began to check their pistols to see if they fired the same caliber ammunition I did. But I was out of luck. My revolver took a .40-caliber shell; all three of the hooded men were carrying .44-caliber pistols.

Two of the men were dead, but one of them was still alive. I didn't have time to mess with him, but I turned him over so he could hear me good and said, "Tell Phil Sharp I ain't through with him. Nor your bunch either."

Then I got out of there and started making my way for the train depot. At first the wound bothered me hardly at all. In fact at first I thought I'd just been grazed. But then, once outside, I saw the blood spreading all over the front of my shirt and I knew that I was indeed hit. I figured I'd been shot by nothing heavier than a .32-caliber revolver but a .32 can kill you just as quick as a cannon if it hits you in the right place.

J.R. ROBERTS
THE
GUNSMITH

If you enjoyed this book, subscribe now and get...

TWO FREE

A $7.00 VALUE–

If you would like to read more of the very best, most exciting, adventurous, action-packed Westerns being published today, you'll want to subscribe to True Value's Western Home Subscription Service.

Each month the editors of True Value will select the 6 very best Westerns from America's leading publishers for special readers like you. You'll be able to preview these new titles as soon as they are published, *FREE* for ten days with no obligation!

TWO FREE BOOKS

When you subscribe, we'll send you your first month's shipment of the newest and best 6 Westerns for you to preview. With your first shipment, two of these books will be yours as our introductory gift to you absolutely *FREE* (a $7.00 value), regardless of what you decide to do. If

you like them, as much as we think you will, keep all six books but pay for just 4 at the low subscriber rate of just $2.75 each. If you decide to return them, keep 2 of the titles as our gift. No obligation.

Special Subscriber Savings

When you become a True Value subscriber you'll save money several ways. First, all regular monthly selections will be billed at the low subscriber price of just $2.75 each. That's at least a savings of $4.50 each month below the publishers price. Second, there is never any shipping, handling or other hidden charges—*Free home delivery.* What's more there is no minimum number of books you must buy, you may return any selection for full credit and you can cancel your subscription at any time. A TRUE VALUE!

A special offer for people who enjoy reading the best Westerns published today.

WESTERNS!

NO OBLIGATION

Mail the coupon below

To start your subscription and receive 2 FREE WESTERNS, fill out the coupon below and mail it today. We'll send your first shipment which includes 2 FREE BOOKS as soon as we receive it.

Mail To: **True Value Home Subscription Services, Inc. P.O. Box 5235
120 Brighton Road, Clifton, New Jersey 07015-5235**

YES! I want to start reviewing the very best Westerns being published today. Send me my first shipment of 6 Westerns for me to preview FREE for 10 days. If I decide to keep them, I'll pay for just 4 of the books at the low subscriber price of $2.75 each; a total $11.00 (a $21.00 value). Then each month I'll receive the 6 newest and best Westerns to preview Free for 10 days. If I'm not satisfied I may return them within 10 days and owe nothing. Otherwise I'll be billed at the special low subscriber rate of $2.75 each; a total of $16.50 (at least a $21.00 value) and save $4.50 off the publishers price. There are never any shipping, handling or other hidden charges. I understand I am under no obligation to purchase any number of books and I can cancel my subscription at any time, no questions asked. In any case the 2 FREE books are mine to keep.

Name _____

Street Address _____ Apt. No. _____

City _____ State _____ Zip Code _____

Telephone _____

Signature _____
(if under 18 parent or guardian must sign)

11045

Terms and prices subject to change. Orders subject
to acceptance by True Value Home Subscription
Services, Inc.